CORRUPTION
A US MARSHAL THRILLER

JODI BURNETT

*For members of the US Marshals Service, both present and past,
that quietly serve our country by hunting dangerous fugitives
and bringing them to justice.*

CORRUPTION

PROLOGUE

He rarely came to Natchitoches. Though his most sumptuous stock was often plucked from the streets of the gentile southern parish, Beaux Crandall preferred to leave the amusement and hardware branches of his business to those in his employ whose lives were steeped in the sticky mire of the seedy side of town.

But that night was different. That night, the high dollar exchange down on Genti Street required his personal supervision.

To pass the time until the transaction, he reviewed his recent batch of videos before they went live. With a single click, the new installment of titillation would zip out, worldwide. Decimal points in his various bank accounts would leap as thousands of anonymous viewers downloaded his offerings. So why did his skin itch? He grew fidgety. Concentration eluded him. The new film footage failed to arouse him.

Beaux checked his watch again. It had been dark for several hours, already. Where the hell was the delivery van? It wasn't like Kenny to be late. Beaux plucked at the sweat-soaked shirt clinging to the folds and creases of his belly.

Headlights swept the faces of the homes across the road as the anticipated moving truck turned onto the pitted street. Slowing, it passed the house, stopped, and then backed into the gravel driveway. It edged underneath the carport at the side of the sad brick house.

"Finally," Beaux murmured leaving the provocative images cavorting on the screen of his laptop. He hoisted his girth out of the chair and left the office to follow his crew outside.

Troy, his personal bodyguard walked beside him. The man was a few inches shorter than Beaux and was built like a Sherman Tank. He'd known Troy since they were boys together in one of the worst group-homes he'd lived in. Troy had been slight then. Several years younger than Beaux. The other kids in the house kicked Troy's ass on a regular basis until Beaux stepped in. He'd saved the little sprout from becoming the delinquent's version of a prison bitch and Troy had been loyal to him ever since.

As they grew, Beaux studied at the underbelly school of crime while Troy took his adolescent rage out at the YMCA gym. Now, they were inseparable. Troy kept him safe and was the only man Beaux trusted.

"What about the earlier shipment, boss?"

"The rifles? We'll take them with us too. This shithole isn't a safe place to keep any of our inventory."

Troy nodded in agreement and led the way out the kitchen door.

The delivery driver rolled up the sliding rear door of the truck as Beaux and his men entered the carport. "Test the crank and let's get out of here. We're already behind schedule. I want this load at the cutting shop before dawn."

A man Beaux nicknamed "Louie," after the chemist Louis Pasteur, stepped forward with his portable cocaine testing kit and waited for the driver to open one of the large square boxes inside the truck. Louie selected and removed a random white brick, sliced the plastic wrapping, and with a small spoon drew a sample. He added the powder to a solution in a clear bottle, capped it and shook. After holding the glass up to the light shining out from the kitchen window, Louie's eyes shifted to Beaux's, and he nodded with a slight smile.

Warm elation flowed through Beaux's veins. This was going to be one of his most profitable hauls so far. "Good. Get the man his money and move this load inside."

"POLICE! FREEZE!" a sharp voice yelled from somewhere in the shadows.

At the command, liquid nitrogen replaced the short-lived heat that seconds ago filled Beaux's system. His body went rigid a breath before Troy threw one arm over Beaux's shoulders, pushed his head down, and ran him into the house.

"Natchitoches PD! Drop your weapons and put your hands on your head!" the voice in the dark ordered.

Troy did not get Beaux through the kitchen before the front door burst open off its hinges and a serpentine line of SWAT officers filed into the living room. Dread pounded inside Beaux's skull. There was no way to escape—nowhere to run. How did the cops know the deal was going down? How long had they been hiding in the shadows?

The lead SWAT officer repeated the order to freeze while his gun-wielding team surrounded Beaux and his guard. Troy dropped his handgun, and both men reluctantly interlaced their fingers on top of their heads.

Officers checked them for weapons. Beaux had no need. He had Troy. After finding a second gun and a knife in an ankle-sheath on his bodyguard, the cops cuffed them both. One of the black-uniformed men read Beaux his rights, but all he could think about was that every branch of his illicit business was currently represented inside this stupid little house. Guns, drugs, and even the child-pornography was open for view on his laptop and the cops would use every item as evidence against him.

"I want to call my attorney," Beaux shouted.

"You can phone him from the station," the officer who cuffed him growled. "Get these dirtbags out of here."

Police escorted Beaux, all his men, and the truck driver to the waiting squad cars. How had they known? Was there a mole in his organization? Hot fury diffused all trace of the cold dread that filled him moments ago. Someone was going to die.

Three Days Later

Beaux Crandall sat next to his long-time attorney, Debbie Hammons. He tapped his fingers on a wooden table that matched the rich paneling in the courtroom, while he waited for the judge to arrive and decide on his proposed bail agreement. Outside, the sky was a slate gray and raindrops splattered against the windows. The dismal weather suited his mood. He wasn't sure how the cops found out about his entrepreneurial extra-curriculars, but his lawyer better be worth her fee on this case. He had no time to waste in jail—he had a business to run.

Beaux drew in a deep breath when the court clerk stood and called out, "All rise. The 10th Judicial District Court of Louisiana is now in session. The Honorable Judge Sadow presiding."

Debbie murmured, "Here we go."

"You better get the job done," Beaux growled under his breath as they rose to their feet with the judge's appearance at the bench.

The old southern justice settled his black-robed backside into the leather chair. "Good morning. Please be seated." A rumble of movement followed as people in the gallery found their seats behind the bar. Beaux ran damp palms down the legs of his suit pants as he lowered his heavy frame into his seat.

The judge continued, "We are here for a bail hearing in the matter of the State of Louisiana versus Beaux Crandall. Mr. Crandall faces charges of money laundering, the sale of illegal firearms, and distribution of child pornography. Assistant District Attorney Gaden, would you care to begin?"

A young, fresh-faced ADA jumped to his feet. "Thank you, Your Honor. Given the severity of the charges, the DA requests that the defendant be held without bail. Mr. Crandall poses a serious flight risk due to the potential penalties he faces upon conviction of the crimes of which he stands accused."

Judge Sadow nodded. "Thank you, counsel. Defense, what is your response?"

Debbie stood. "Thank you, Your Honor. We recognize the severity of the charges but assert my client's innocence.

Mr. Crandall is a lifelong resident of Natchitoches Parish. He has family, friends, and business acquaintances here. The DA has not charged him with any violent crimes, and he does not pose a flight risk, nor a danger to the community. We propose a suitable bail and agree to any pre-trial conditions Your Honor requests to ensure Mr. Crandall's appearance at future court proceedings."

Leafing through the papers on his desk, the judge asked, "Does Mr. Crandall have any prior criminal history?"

"No, sir." Debbie offered the judge an earnest smile. "This is his first encounter with the law." Beaux resisted scoffing. He had a highly dubious past to be sure, but nothing that remained in any official records.

"I see. Considering the severity of the criminal charges Mr. Crandall faces, in contrast with his lack of criminal history, community ties, local business, and your proposed bail and pre-trial conditions, I am inclined to grant bail in the amount of one-million dollars. Mr. Crandall, you must adhere to the following conditions: You are to have no contact with any potential witnesses or alleged victims in this case."

Beaux conjured up his best innocent-choir-boy expression and nodded at the judge's orders as he continued, "You may not leave the boundaries of the 10th Judicial District Court of Louisiana. You will surrender your passport to the Louisiana Pretrial Services. You will report to those same services on a weekly basis until your trial, and you are not to commit any new offenses while on release."

The judge glowered at him over the rim of his reading glasses. "Failure to adhere to all of these conditions will result in bail revocation and your detention in the county jail until your trial. Do you understand these conditions, Mr. Crandall?"

Beaux swallowed solemnly. "Yes, Your Honor. I understand."

"Very well. This hearing is adjourned." Judge Sadow followed his statement with a solid rap of his gavel.

Beaux held a firm grip on his glee and the grin that tickled his lips and shook Debbie's hand. "Thank you, Debbie. Next, I need you to put my plantation home up for collateral on the bail, and I'll see to it you are well compensated."

"I'd rather you took me with you wherever you are going," she murmured. "This could be the end of my law career here in Natchitoches."

"Whatever are you talking about?" Beaux smiled beatifically and batted his eyes. He glanced sideways at the people in the gallery. Some had been there to witness his arraignment and bail hearing, but most were present for upcoming cases. Troy stood at the back of the room waiting for him, having been recently released on a bail agreement of his own. "If you'll excuse me, Debbie, I have a lunch meeting to attend. Thank you for your excellent work here today. I'll be in touch."

"Right." Debbie slid her files into the briefcase and followed him out the courtroom doors.

One Year Later

Beaux stood on the deck of an exquisite timber home he'd been living in since he jumped bail and escaped to Patuanak, Saskatchewan. The place belonged on the cover of Log Cabin Home Magazine. It had six bedrooms, each with its own full bath. He enjoyed a gourmet kitchen, and the view of a sky-blue Canadian lake from the great room was rivaled by none. Beaux sipped from a cup of steaming black coffee while a majestic bald eagle spread his wings and cascaded from the sky toward the pristine lake fifty yards away. The graceful bird reached his powerful talons into the pool and scooped up a flopping trout for breakfast as a second eagle's cry echoed across the water.

A client of Beaux's, who didn't want his steady stream of pornography to dry up, owned the cabin. He had offered it to Beaux for as long as he needed a place to hide in return for full access to Beaux's video library. And it had been the perfect spot to hole up while he plotted his next move. The magnificent view helped to soothe his growing edginess, but the isolation was grating.

These days, Beaux's patience wore as thin as the icy northern air surrounding him. He had no intention of staying through another freezing season in this god-forsaken wilderness. He had, however, come to love the beauty and peace of mountain life; all he wanted was to be warmer. Besides, he couldn't run his business effectively from such a remote Northern Canadian location for much longer. He longed to return to the United States where he was in the thick of things and corrupt money flowed like a fountain into his coffers.

He went back inside the mansion to search on his computer for ranches on the market in Montana. He was eager to return to work full-time. Within an hour, he had several realtors on the job looking for the perfect mountain property. Next, he called his munitions dealer. Step one was to assess his current money-making venture—the one that would fund his new home.

After what he had determined was a long enough period of silence following his escape, he had ordered a shipment of semiautomatic rifles with detachable magazines and telescoping stocks. He arranged for the guns to travel up from Mexico to Wyoming. There was always a healthy gun market in the western states, and naturally, word spread to like-minded buyers in Washington, Idaho, and across all the northern border states to Wisconsin.

He punched a number into his phone. "Hey. It's me. What's the status of my order?"

"Señor Crandall. First, don't panic. Everything's under control."

Ice-water sluiced through Beaux's body and pooled in his gut even as white-hot heat boiled his blood and filled his head with steam. "What the hell are you talking about?"

"The buyer in Wyoming called and said the shipment never showed, but I'm sure it's just a glitch in the travel arrangements. I've been trying to get ahold of our contact."

"Didn't show? What the hell happened? Where are my guns?"

"Señor, stay calm. I will fix this."

"It's your life if you don't!" Beaux slammed his phone onto the granite kitchen counter ending the call. His screen shattered. "Troy!" he yelled for his bodyguard.

The heavily muscled man, dressed in black cargo pants and a winter-weight Under Armour shirt, ran into the room with his pistol drawn. "Sir, what's wrong?"

"We must go to Wyoming immediately. The gun shipment never arrived. We need to calm our buyer down and find out what happened before all hell breaks loose!"

Troy reseated his weapon in his shoulder holster. "I'll call your pilot right away."

Troy would attend to all the travel arrangements, but it would be up to Beaux himself to de-escalate the situation. He mourned the old network he had built in Louisiana before he had been arrested; a band of men he trusted to deal with these kinds of details and problems. "And Troy, locate those guns!"

After Troy nodded and jogged out of the room to perform his tasks, Beaux called for the housekeeper to pack his bag. He and Troy would be on their way south, back to the lucrative United States of America, within the hour.

Troy had arranged for a private plane to fly them to a remote spot near the US border. From there they hiked across the border and met a man hired to fly them in a helicopter to Sheridan, Wyoming. Beaux had a contact there who lent them a car. From there they drove east into the countryside to the location where Beaux's gun deal was supposed to take place.

When they arrived at the pre-arranged meeting location in the wilds of Wyoming, Troy parked the black Cadillac and jumped out to open Beaux's door for him. Wind whipped around them as they walked toward a rusty, corrugated-tin structure. The building's flaking turquoise door was flanked by two darkened windows, one of which had a crack that spanned the distance between corners. A strong gust whistled through the brush on the dry ground and Beaux had to lean into its force to walk forward.

A deep voice called out from inside the building stopping them in their tracks. "Hold up! Take off your coats and show me your hands!"

Beaux nodded to Troy, and they complied. "Listen, I came here myself when I heard there was a problem with the shipment. I am currently looking into what happened and will see that you get your product as soon as possible."

"My boss expected those guns yesterday. He has some very important buyers waiting, and they aren't the kind of men you want to piss off."

"No, of course not, which is why I came here personally." Beaux smiled placatingly, even though he was furious that he'd had to attend to this issue himself. The task was beneath him. But he hadn't yet had time to construct a trustworthy network in this part of the country to deal with complications like this. It was the next thing on his list, but he needed the funds from this shipment to accomplish it. He slid out of his suit coat and held it aloft in one hand. Troy did the same with his tactical jacket.

"Throw your weapons on the ground."

Troy's shoulder holster was visible to the man inside screaming the orders, so he complied by tossing that handgun onto the dirt. Beaux didn't move. He was armed, but there was no way in hell he was going to give up any weapons that the man couldn't see.

"Now step away from the gun," the disembodied voice yelled. Beaux and Troy moved several steps from Troy's pistol and a tall, wiry man with long graying-black hair came out from behind the building. He aimed a semiautomatic rifle at them—one exactly like the guns in the expected shipment. "My boss agreed to do business with you because someone he trusted gave him your name. But he can't trust *you*, can he? In this business, men like you don't last."

Beaux raised open hands. "The fact that I came to you personally proves that I *am* trustworthy. I'm here to ask for a couple of days to find out what happened, and then we'll get your merchandise to you. I'm certain there was a simple, minor delay."

"If the shipment is on its way, then what do I need you for?" The man fired a single shot into the ground near Beaux's feet.

Beaux refused to flinch. "I don't appreciate you threatening me. Especially when I came here in good faith."

"Well, I don't appreciate you putting me in this position. A group of angry, deadly men want their guns." The man raised the sight on his rifle and peered through it at Beaux's head.

From the corner of his eye, Beaux caught Troy's movement a half-second before he tackled Beaux to the ground. Simultaneously, Troy pulled a gun from his low-back holster and fired at the armed man. The man returned the shots, but his aim was wide. Troy kept his trigger compressed, and his automatic pistol launched bullets until his magazine emptied. The buyer's shoulder exploded with blood and bone, and he screamed out in pain. His body then jerked with each ensuing round until he lay dead in the dirt, soaking in his own gore.

Beaux pushed himself to his feet and brushed dust from his shirt. "Well done, Troy. But did you have to get my suit dirty?" He laughed at his own joke.

Troy pulled the empty magazine from his gun and replaced it with a fresh one. "What do you want me to do with him, boss?"

"Look inside. See if there's anything we can stuff him in."

Troy holstered his pistol and after bending to retrieve the gun he had tossed on the ground, he jogged inside. Minutes later he returned. "We're in luck. There's an empty wooden rifle-crate in there. Like the ones we use for our shipments."

Beaux scrunched his face in on itself. "That rat bastard. He probably sold my guns and then claimed they never showed up." Wrinkle by wrinkle, he grinned with a delightful sense of wickedness. "The chest is perfect. Cram his body in there, and I'll leave a note."

He located a scrap of paper in the car and jotted a message: *"To whom this may concern. I guarantee your merchandise will arrive at our agreed upon secondary emergency location, next Friday. I apologize for the delay. But from now on, understand that I do not respond well to minions stealing my inventory or threats of any kind. Sincerely, Your New Supplier."* After penning his note, Beaux found a hammer. He pulled a new four-inch nail from the stash he liked to keep in his shirt pocket and tacked the paper to the dead man's forehead. The cracking sound of the sharp metal piercing bone filled Beaux's senses with pleasure.

"Let's grab some lunch, I'm famished. After that, I have some properties to see up in Montana. It's high time I found a place to land and got my business up and running again. I've really missed the work and I want to be near enough to the supply chain to keep a closer eye on the merchandise." Troy nodded and opened the car door for Beaux. "And, Troy, call around. We'll need some new kids and a studio to make fresh videos at our new home." He rested his hands on his hips and turned in a slow circle.

"Everything is lining up nicely for my re-entry into the United States. All the ranches I'm looking at are within a hundred miles of Reservation casinos—which will provide the perfect solution for washing our colorful new income."

Beaux sucked in a great breath of fresh air and as he lowered himself into the Cadillac he sang, "I'm ba-ack."

CHAPTER 1

irk Sterling clicked on the desktop computer that took up most of his desk in the US Marshals Office in Billings, Montana. A photo of him and his now deceased partner, Sam Dillinger, filled the monitor. They had been on a fishing trip together when they took the selfie. Dirk had a carousel of photos set up for his screen saver, and this one always made him smile even as it weighed down his heart. He missed the man, more than he liked to admit.

"Sterling." His boss, Chief Emory Grey's voice came from directly behind him.

Startled, he clicked off the image, and arranging his features into a coy grin, he spun around in his chair. He looked up at the beautiful, no-nonsense blonde woman standing over him. "What can I do for you, Chief?"

Her long, elegant neck made it obvious when she swallowed nervously. He liked that he still made her uneasy, even though she had moved on and was now dating Dave Aldrich—the dweeb FBI agent they'd worked with on their last big case. Okay, so maybe he wasn't really a dweeb, but still.

"I was going over today's blotter, and I read about a gun smuggling deal gone wrong down in Wyoming. A sheriff's deputy saw some suspicious cars leaving an old Quonset hut on an abandoned property in his county. He investigated the building and found a dead man crammed into a wooden crate with a note nailed to his forehead. The note apologizes for a delay and then promises to make it up. It's signed, 'Your new supplier.'"

"That's gruesome, but what does it have to do with us? Do you think the perp has an outstanding federal warrant, or something?"

"I think there's a good chance."

"Do you want me to hunt this guy down?"

"Yes. You and Henry."

"What about the Deputy Marshals in Wyoming? Won't they want to handle this? I know if my friend, Reed, hears about it, she'll be all over the case."

"*If* the suspect is in Wyoming, you'd be right. But since the deputy found the body in the wilderness close to the north Wyoming border, the killer might be somewhere else. He could just as easily be in Montana or South Dakota, and I want *our* team to catch him."

"I'm on it." Dirk spun around to face his computer. He pecked on his keyboard with two fingers bringing up the case in the news. "Where is Hank, by the way? That schoolboy is never late to work."

Emory pursed her lips. "He'll be here soon. He had to attend to a personal matter."

Dirk glanced over his shoulder to see if he could catch her expression, but he only caught a blonde flair as she turned to go to her office. He noticed Teresa, the team admin, watching him. She wore her black hair pulled into two braids tied together in the back.

"What's up with Hank?" he asked her.

She shrugged. "I don't know. He called about an hour ago wanting to talk to the chief."

"Is he sick or something?"

"Didn't sound sick. Either way, he'll be in later this morning. Why?"

"Just wondered. It's not like him to miss a second of work, that's all."

Teresa pushed away from her desk and after glancing at Emory's door, lowered her voice. "I think it's *because* he hates missing any work."

"What do you mean?"

"His wife calls him all the time, and I heard him talking to her in the break room one day. He sounded angry and was saying something about this being his job, and if he didn't come to work, they couldn't pay their bills."

"Is he having financial trouble?" Dirk didn't like talking about his new partner behind his back. He didn't enjoy talking about people in general. But he was worried about Hank.

"I don't think so. In my opinion, Amy—that's his wife —just hates how many hours he puts in."

Dirk chuffed. "Well, she shouldn't have married a US Marshal then. It's not like this is a nine-to-five. And he was in the Army before that. You'd think she would be used to odd hours."

"I don't know, but whatever's going on is serious enough for Hank to call out for the morning."

"Hm." Dirk returned to his research. He read the police

report and glanced through the attached photos. The file told the same story Emory had and there were few relevant details beyond the nail through the skull. But the nail had no useful fingerprints, and the victim was a John Doe so far. Dirk flipped through the pictures one more time. People did the most heinous shit to each other.

He went to the FBI's ViCap database which housed various types of modus operandi, signature aspects, crime scene descriptions, and images. It also included details about the victims and suspects, along with an analysis of violent and sexual crimes. If there was more than one instance of someone nailing messages to their victim's head, he would find it in there.

He came upon a man named Crandall who had been arrested in Louisiana over a year ago, suspected of money laundering, gunrunning, and the distribution of child pornography. Apparently, after they released the man on bail, he disappeared, which made him a person of interest for the Marshals.

Sub-notes added by the FBI mentioned several incidents where cops found victims with paper notes nailed to their heads. With a jolt, Dirk sat forward and scrolled on through the report. The unusual MO implied Crandall was possibly connected to the murders.

The evidence the prosecutor in Louisiana had presented was solid. Crandall must have had a sharp attorney to get the judge to allow for bail at all. Dirk read through the court documents before he moved on to the investigation report where he opened a PDF titled *The Playground*. Past the front page was a table of contents, which looked like a list of childhood games—Duck-Duck-Goose, Chutes and Ladders, Candy Land, and more. He clicked the arrow to the next page, and he was confronted with a grid of photos.

Thirty little faces stared out at him. Both boys and girls, none older than thirteen and some as young as three inhabited the pictures causing Dirk's brows to crunch together. He was certain he did not want to see what followed the introductory pages, but if children were being abused, someone had to help them. He clenched his jaw and breathed in through his nose, held his breath and clicked to the next page.

What he saw curdled his stomach. Images of children forced into adult sexual acts flooded his screen. In some photos the kids were with each other, in others, they were with adults whose faces someone had blurred out. Dirk closed the document and shoved his chair away from his desk. He jumped to his feet, filled with a sickened raw rage. How could anyone do such horrible things to innocent kids?

"You, okay?" Teresa asked.

"Not really," he murmured as he stalked to the water cooler in the break room. He filled a glass with ice-water and chugged it down.

Teresa was hot on his heels. "What's going on, Sterling?"

"I just got an eyeful of what some sick puke is doing to children and then posting the videos for sale on the dark web." His anger demanded an outlet, and he slammed his open hand against a cupboard.

The loud noise brought Emory rushing into the room. "What happened?" Concern filled her green eyes. "Did something fall?"

Abashed at his lack of control, Dirk muttered, "Nothing. Sorry. I just got a dose of some real twisted crap." He told her what he'd seen on the FBI's site.

Emory's voice softened, and she placed her hand on his shoulder in comfort. "It must have been horrific."

"Yeah." He closed his eyes and focused on his breath. "I was searching for the nailed-note MO and came across a man named Beaux Crandall. He's a fugitive who jumped bail in Louisiana a year ago." He told her all that he discovered.

"So, you're thinking that the guy dealing guns in Wyoming might be this Beaux Crandall?"

"Sure could be. But either way, I want to work on his case. We have to find him and stop him from hurting kids."

"I'll call Agent Aldrich and see what he can find out on the FBI's end."

Dirk side-eyed her but kept his thoughts about Aldrich to himself. The fact that his case gave Emory an excuse to bring in the FBI agent didn't sit well in his already upset gut.

Emory continued, "At this point, we're only sticking our toes into the investigation. The gun deal might come from somewhere else altogether."

"We still need to find Crandall and take him down." He glowered at her.

She lifted her hand from his shoulder, letting her fingers linger long enough to burn his skin under their pressure. "If the perp is one and the same, then good. Otherwise, the Crandall case will have to wait."

He shrugged off the urge to grasp her hand and instead moved away from her to look out the window. "When did Hank say he was going to be here?"

"After lunch."

"Teresa." He swung his gaze to her. "Get him on the phone and tell him to get here as soon as he can." The admin glanced at their boss and then returned to her desk.

"Dirk..." Emory started to say something, but then rolled her lips between her teeth as if that would keep them closed.

He raised his brows in question. "Dirk... what?"

She lifted her chin. "Leave Henry alone, this morning. He needs some personal time and we're going to give it to him. Is that clear?" Without waiting for his response, she raised her voice and called, "Teresa, don't bother calling Henry. He'll be in the office soon enough."

"What's going on, Emory?" What wasn't she telling him? "Is Hank, okay?"

"That's *Chief* to you, and yes. Henry is fine. He'll talk to you about it if he wants to. Otherwise, give him some space."

Dirk met her gaze straight on, mildly stunned at her reproof. "Sorry, Chief. *Surely*, you understand that I'm just concerned about him." He used the word that was synonymous with the false name she gave him when they first met. Before they knew she was his new boss, she'd had too much to drink and came on to him in a honky-tonk up in the mountains. She'd told him her name was "Shirley". Now, whenever he wanted to get a rise out of her, he applied the synonym hoping to see pink bloom in her cheeks.

Emory narrowed her eyes and the blush he was hoping for never rose. "And that's enough of the Shirley business, too." She spun on her sensible, stout heels and stalked out of the break room.

It was turning out to be a shitty morning, so Dirk pulled out his phone and called his only other trusted friend in the world—Caitlyn Reed.

"Hey, Dirk. What's up?"

"Want to hunt down a sleazebag with me?"

"Of course, I do. But I'm grounded for a little while. Renegade is in, practicing for the annual re-qual for his certification as a US Marshal K9. McKenzie has been training with him. Of course, she's secretly getting Ren to spend time with her Malinois, Athena, so they'll breed together. Ha! Who are you hunting?"

It was good to hear Caitlyn's voice. He had always liked working with her and her dog Renegade. She was tough as rawhide and never minced words about anything. Caitlyn was a what-you-see-is-what-you-get kind of person, which is why he wanted to touch base with her now. He felt like his world was tilting sideways lately with his unwanted feelings for Emory, not to mention his confused emotions regarding his dead partner's widow, Laurie. And now he had to worry about his *new* partner. What the hell was happening?

"Just a money laundering, gun smuggling, child porn pervert."

"Oh, the usual, then." Caitlyn chuckled.

"Yeah. Well, if you can't work, you want to meet at the gun range, then? I mean, if you're sloughing off, the least you can do is keep your aim sharp."

"I can always out-shoot you, Sterling."

"We'll see. Put your money where your mouth is. Loser buys dinner and beers."

"You're on."

After they made plans to join up at their favorite gun

range half-way between Billings and Moose Creek, Wyoming, Dirk felt lighter. Why couldn't all relationships be as easy and straightforward as his friendship with Caitlyn?

At 11:20 am, Hank entered the office. He didn't meet Dirk's eye and his usual happy-go-lucky attitude was nowhere to be seen. Dirk rolled his chair across the room to Hank's desk. "What's up, kid?"

Two angry red blotches appeared on Hank's cheekbones. He shrugged. "Nothing. Did I miss anything this morning?"

"Grey wants us to look into a shooting down in Wyoming. It might have something to do with a bail-jumper from Louisiana who was up for money laundering, gunrunning, and child porn."

"And he showed up in Montana?"

"Maybe. It's hard to say. It's the FBI's case so I don't have all the details."

Hank, keeping his eyes cast downward, nodded. He opened and then closed his desk drawer and moved his pen jar from one side of his workspace to the other.

"Listen, kid. You don't have to tell me what's going on with you, but I'm here if you decide you want to talk."

———

Emory observed her team through the open crack of her office door as soon as Henry arrived. His face was pale and drawn, and he couldn't seem to find a comfortable place for his hands to rest, moving them from his pockets, through his hair, to his hips. Poor kid. And now, he had to face his hero and mentor.

She could only hope Dirk had a sensitive side. She had glimpsed what she believed might be a little vulnerability in him when they all thought they were going to die in a helicopter crash over Lake Ontario during one of their big cases. But maybe that was just imagination on her part. She hadn't seen it again since then.

Her phone buzzed from on top of her desk. The caller ID informed her it was Agent Aldrich. "Dave, hi." Her greeting caused Dirk to turn his attention toward her office, so she leaned over and closed the door.

"Hello, beautiful. I got your message, what's up?"

"Have you ever heard of a man called Beaux Crandall? He's a fugitive who jumped bail in Louisiana a little over a year ago."

"No, should I have?"

"Well, maybe. He's been on the FBI's most-wanted list since then. I'm sure you've probably seen his face. Either way, they arrested Crandall for money laundering, sale of illegal firearms, and distribution of child pornography."

"Ah, a definite dirt bag."

"Yes. Well, they awarded him a million-dollar bail down in Natchitoches Parish, Louisiana, and after he put his house up as collateral and paid the money, he skipped out on it. There has been no record of him in the United States since."

"Until now?"

"I'm not sure. I had Dirk looking into a gun smuggling case in northern Wyoming, and he followed the crumbs to Crandall. Would you look into the guy from your end and see what you can turn up?"

"Are you asking as a Chief Deputy US Marshal or as a… friend?"

"At this point, as a friend. I just want to see if there is any weight to what Dirk discovered. He was upset by some of the child pornography he saw on the ViCap database."

"You're *always* looking out for him," he complained.

"Of course, I am," she defended. "That's my job. And I hope you're not insinuating something other than that."

"Okay, okay. Don't get pissed at me. It's just... never mind. I'm happy to poke around and let you know if I find anything interesting."

"Thank you."

"Now that we've got that business out of the way, what are you doing after work? Want to meet for drinks, or I could take you to dinner?"

"Sure, drinks would be nice. O'Malley's?" Drinks were safer. Dinner left her open to Dave wanting to drive and then fishing for an invitation to come up to her apartment when he took her home. It wasn't unreasonable of him. They'd been seeing each other for a while, now. But she wasn't ready. She had too many unresolved feelings to sort through. Feelings, if she were honest with herself, for Dirk. Why could she not shake that man?

CHAPTER 2

Dirk studied Hank from across the room. The kid looked miserable and for some reason wouldn't meet his eye. Dirk decided not to bring up the obvious fact that Hank was struggling with something. If he wanted to talk, he would.

"Now that you're here, Hank, are you ready to check out that gun smuggling case in Wyoming? I emailed you my notes, but I thought we might want to drive down to Johnson County and check out the crime scene for ourselves."

Hank tapped all ten fingers on the edge of his desk like he was playing an imaginary piano. "Today? What time would we get back?"

Dirk cocked his head. "When we're done."

The kid checked his watch. "Maybe Teresa could go with you on this one?"

"Teresa has to pick up her kid after work." Something was definitely wrong in Hank's world, so Dirk let off the pressure. "But don't worry about it. If you have something going on, I'll run down there on my own. I wanted to meet Reed at the gun range anyway, maybe she can do it today."

"I'm sorry, Sterling." Hank glanced up at him then, but shifted his gaze away again.

"No apology necessary. But we are partners, you know. If you need to get something off your chest, you can."

Hank nodded, but instead of answering, he clicked on his computer and opened Dirk's email.

Dirk shot a look at Teresa who lifted her brows and shrugged. He grabbed his phone and sent a text to Caitlyn. **Any chance ur free tonight? Or do you need time to practice before I kick your ass?**

After several minutes, she responded. **You wish! Mind if Colt comes? Then when you lose, you can buy him dinner too.**

Dirk chuckled, happy to have plans with good friends. **You're on. See u guys at 6.** He shoved his phone into his back pocket and grabbed his keys. Stopping at Emory's door, he knocked.

"Come in."

He opened the door halfway and leaned around it. "I'm going down to the crime scene in Wyoming. See if I find anything besides what's already in the reports. Figure I'll talk to the deputy who found the dead guy."

"Are you taking Hank?"

"No."

"I'd like the two of you to work this case together."

"I know, but he's got something going on."

Emory hesitated. "Did he tell you anything?"

It was Dirk's turn to pause. What the hell was up? "Look, I don't know what's got Hank's jockeys in a twist, but I'm not going to beg him to talk to me like some teenaged girl. You clearly know what it is, so *you* talk to him. I have work to do." He turned to leave.

"Dirk."

He stopped but didn't turn back.

"Keep me informed."

"I'll call you when I get home."

"I—uh. I have plans tonight. So, unless it's urgent, we can discuss the case tomorrow."

"You and Aldrich?" Now that Emory had a thing for the agent, it seemed the dude was everywhere. He was always with Emory, and now in the middle of Dirk's case-work too.

"Not that it's any of your business."

He faced her then. "Used to be, in this office, the team was like a family. Everybody cared enough about each other and trusted each other to share their lives. Guess things have changed, since you got here." Dirk closed Emory's office door behind him, and walked toward the exit.

"Hey, Sterling, hold up." Hank got up from his desk and slid his phone into his coat pocket. "I'll come with you."

Damn. He didn't mean to guilt the kid into coming. He had meant his barbed comment purely for Emory. For some stupid reason, he let her relationship with Aldrich get to him. "It's fine. I get it if you have something you gotta do."

"I worked it out. It's okay." Hank walked past him out the office door. "I'll drive."

"I'm meeting Reed and her husband for a round of shooting and dinner after."

"Mind if I tag along?"

Dirk shook his head at the change in his partner's mood. "No, but if you're the worst shot, you're buying dinner for four."

Hank laughed. "I can't afford it, so I guess I'll just need to beat you."

Dirk chuckled and gave an internal shrug, relieved to be back on level ground. "Not a chance."

On the drive down to Wyoming, the partners discussed the murder and the possibility of Crandall being involved. The crime scene was no longer taped off when they arrived. So, they walked the lot and searched through the Quonset hut.

Hank moved to the center of the building. "This would make an ideal structure to store crates of guns, or anything else someone wanted to hide, and the location is the epitome of BFE. A smuggler could drive his truck in through the back door, unload, and leave again, with no one the wiser."

"Only, in this case, the guns never arrived." Dirk pointed to a row of what looked like offices along one wall. "Let's check those rooms. See if it looks like somebody lives here or if it's only used for business."

Dirk started on the right side, and Hank jogged to the left. The first room he came to was a utility closet. Whoever owned the building probably designed the next several rooms as offices, only they were mostly empty. He and Hank met in the middle. This center space was two rooms made into one. Inside, there were three couches, a huge TV hooked to a game system, and a refrigerator. Dirk opened the fridge door. "Beer and more beer. This must be where the runners wait for their deals to go down."

The building's exterior door slammed shut, causing both Dirk and Hank to draw their weapons and take cover.

"Whoever's in here, come out with your hands over your head!" a man shouted from inside the hut.

"US Marshals. Who are you?" Dirk yelled back from behind the wall.

"I'm gonna need to see some IDs. Real slow."

"Who are you?"

"I'm the sheriff in these parts. Sheriff Murdoch. If you're US Marshals, why the hell didn't you call my office before you started poking around? Now hold your hands over your heads with your credentials and come out, real slow."

Dirk gestured to Hank to stay behind while he went out to meet the man claiming to be the sheriff. He mouthed, "Cover me."

Hank bobbed his head. Dirk holstered his weapon and pushed his leather jacket back to reveal the silver-star badge attached to his belt. He held his billfold in the air with his ID showing and stepped from the room. In the center of the building, where he could have easily been shot, stood a middle-aged man in a tan-and-brown sheriff's uniform. He held his gun in both hands, pointing it at Dirk.

"I'd appreciate it if you'd lower your weapon, Sheriff. I'm Deputy US Marshal Dirk Sterling from the Billings office."

The lawman jammed his pistol back into his holster as Dirk approached. He took Dirk's billfold and studied the ID. "So, tell me. What are a couple of feds from Montana doing poking around down here in Wyoming?" He returned Dirk's identification.

"Come on out, Hank." Dirk enjoyed the startled look on the sheriff's face when Hank stepped from the room. "Next time you find yourself in a situation like this, Sheriff, you might want to take cover before you order a person to come out of hiding. If we were bad guys, you'd already be dead."

The sheriff glowered at him. "I'll ask again. What are you two doing down here in Wyoming?"

Dirk explained why they were there looking at the crime scene and the likelihood of the culpable arms dealer hiding out in Montana or South Dakota. "The way your deputy found the victim with a note tacked to his head matches the MO of a fugitive we're interested in. We'd love to follow you back to your office and have a look at the investigation notes you have so far."

"I'm sure you would. But I was on my way out when I saw your truck parked here. I'm not going back to the office tonight."

"Fair enough. Mind if we go into town without you and look at the report?"

"Ours is a very small town. We don't man the office twenty-four seven. No one will be there until around ten tomorrow morning."

"There a place to stay?"

"Yeah. There's the Big Horn Inn on Main Street."

Dirk slid his wallet back into his jeans pocket. "Guess we'll see you in the morning, then."

"No need. I can have my deputy email you any pertinent information."

"That would be great, but I still want to talk to the

deputy who found the victim, and I'd like to speak with him in person."

"Suit yourselves. I'm late for dinner with friends, though, so I'm outta here." He walked toward the door and then paused. "That means you two are leaving too."

"We're still assessing the scene. Don't worry, Sheriff. We'll lock up when we go." The sheriff's mouth opened and closed. He shifted his weight and crossed his arms obviously uncomfortable with Dirk and Hank staying behind. "It's okay, we're professionals. We won't bother anything your deputies may have missed."

In response to that comment, Sheriff Murdoch clamped his jaw shut and harrumphed before he exited the building through the turquoise door.

Hank smirked. "Making friends and influencing people as usual, huh Sterling?"

"What was up with that guy? It's not as though we're the criminals around here." Dirk returned to the office they hadn't yet scrutinized. "Doesn't look like much more than a well-stocked breakroom, to me."

"Me either." Hank reached for the gaming system and clicked on the TV. "Whoever hangs out here was playing Gears of War. It's a pretty graphic game, but that doesn't necessarily mean anything."

"We might have better luck talking to some people in town. Looks like we'll need to spend the night down here, anyway."

Hank turned away, but not before Dirk took in his rock-hard jawline. "I thought you said we'd be home tonight."

"I did, but that was before I found out the Sheriff's

office closes at five. What's up? Is Amy gonna give you shit about not coming home?"

"Count on it."

"Best to bite the bullet and call her now. Blame it on me. I'm the one who decided to stay."

"Oh, I will." A brief smile tugged at Hank's mouth before he slid his phone from his pants pocket and tapped on the screen.

Dirk left the room to give the kid some privacy. He zig-zagged across the dirt floor of the building outside of the offices and took the opportunity to shoot Caitlyn a text cancelling their plans. Tires from a large vehicle had left marks in the sand. Near the back double sliding doors, he found the imprint of two parallel thin tires and a smaller track in the middle. It occurred to him then why someone had built a Quonset hut out in the middle of nowhere.

He started to call for Hank but heard the kid's voice rise behind the office door. Congratulating himself, once again, on his decision to remain single, Dirk waited until the conversation cooled. Hank finally stepped out of the room.

"Sorry about that."

"None of my business." Dirk noticed the war-worn shadows lurking in Hank's eyes. "Listen, I'm gonna have to cancel with Caitlyn and Colt at this point, anyway. Let's head home, and I'll drive back down here tomorrow on my own."

"Nah. It's okay, this is our job."

"Yeah, but Amy's your wife." He started toward Hank's truck. "And believe me, it's never good when your wife hates your work."

Hank jogged to catch up. "I want to stay here and

finish what we've started. Amy will eventually understand."

"Are you sure?"

"I am." Hank walked backward next to Dirk and looked him in the eye. "Were you ever married?"

Dirk picked up his pace and Hank had to turn around to keep up. He had no intention of visiting his past. "Once. But not long enough for me to give any advice. Let's head into town and grab some dinner. Maybe some locals will share gossip about the case. Somebody has to know something."

CHAPTER 3

Hank hurried after Dirk. He'd come to realize during the short time he'd spent as Sterling's partner that asking about the man's personal life never went well. The guy was totally closed off, but Hank needed some counsel. He respected Dirk and hoped to gain some wisdom from him. He said he was married once, which meant he was divorced. Or widowed. Crap. Hopefully, he hadn't brought up painful memories.

They bounced along the two-track dirt road back to pavement and then turned left toward town. Dirk rested his booted foot on the dash as he texted his friends. Hank set the cruise control and ventured out on a personal note. "Amy has a hard time understanding our work hours."

"I gathered that." Dirk finished with his phone and put it away. "Were you two married when you were on active duty?"

"During my last year. But I was an MP in Germany then, and for the most part, I had a regular schedule. Amy was friends with a bunch of Army wives too, and they traveled all over Europe together. It was different."

"Yeah, there aren't any other Deputy Marshal's wives around."

"Right. She hasn't made any friends in Billings yet, and you and I have been on the road a lot."

Dirk kept his gaze out the windshield and nodded. "Loneliness is a real thing."

Hank's chest tightened with compassion both for the haunted tone in Dirk's comment and for Amy. His wife was quiet and didn't make friends as easily as he did. "I get it, but I can't be her only person. It's too much sometimes."

"You could get a dog."

"That's what *I* said, but Amy wants a baby."

Dirk's eyes closed, and his Adam's apple bobbed up and down his throat. He rested his head back against the seat but said nothing. Hank had bumped into some deep, private pain that his partner carried.

They were almost to town when Dirk cleared his throat. "Do you want kids too?"

"Yeah, sure I do, but..."

Dirk opened his eyes and shifted his gaze to Hank. "But... what?"

He didn't want to say the next words out loud, but he pressed on, "We've been trying for over a year. But I'm gone a lot, and it seems like it's always at times when Amy is, you know. Ready."

"And tonight is one of those nights?"

"I guess. But you and I didn't know we'd have to stay overnight."

"No, but you could have gone home. I told you it

wasn't a big deal."

Hank couldn't argue with Dirk's logic. The man was right. How could he explain his feelings when he didn't understand them himself? He loved Amy. And he wanted kids, too. But the constant pressure and nagging about sex at just the right time was killing something between them. Most guys would be thrilled if their wives called them and told them to hurry home for a quickie. But with the command performances, the constant medical exams, and temperature taking, all of it made him feel like a trained monkey—or at least something less than a man. Unlike his job, which was exciting—an adrenaline rush—a place where he felt he made a real difference in the world.

Hank sighed. "I know, but this is important too. I care about my career. Amy and me, we just have to find a good balance, that's all."

Dirk pointed out the windshield. "There's the town. Let's check into the inn and then find the local diner."

"Sounds good. I'm starving." Hank flipped the indicator—the clicking reminding him of a countdown timer.

———

Dirk was relieved to see the town. Their conversation was bumping too close to a whole closet of emotions he'd padlocked shut and stuffed deep into the dark recesses of his soul. "There's the inn. Up on the left."

Hank turned into the empty lot. "Looks like we're the only ones here."

"It's not as though this is a big tourist destination."

They checked in and then walked down the two blocks of Main Street. It was a quaint little berg with a coffee shop and a bookstore nestled between a post office and an antique shop. Dirk noted the Sheriff's Office across the street next to an old church the town had converted into a library. The only restaurant they found open wasn't a diner after all, but a Mexican place with a bar.

The conversations of the few people inside halted when they walked through the door. The bartender recovered the quickest. "Howdy, boys. You here for drinks or dinner?"

"Both," Dirk answered. "Something smells fantastic." He breathed in a spicy, fried aroma.

"Take a seat anywhere. Juanita will be with you in a sec."

"Thanks." Dirk led the way. Hank followed him, along with all the eyes in the room.

They sat at a table near the back, taking seats that faced the bar and the front door. Hank leaned close. "Think we stand out?" He grinned.

Dirk's young partner, with his blond hair and millennial good looks, stood out in this place like a southern Californian surfer at a small-town rodeo. "Nah, you fit right in."

Juanita, who reminded him of one of the German women at the Hofbräuhaus who could carry three, liter-sized steins in each hand, arrived at their table. The only difference was she had black hair and dark eyes instead of blonde and blue. "What can I get you?"

Both men ordered a pint of beer and asked for menus. When the waitress returned, Dirk read over the sticky laminated food list and asked for a smothered burrito. He waited for Hank to order before he asked, "Hey Juanita, is there an airport anywhere around here?"

She laughed a great belly laugh. "Are you kidding, mister? The closest airports to this town are in Sheridan and Gillette. Public airports, anyway."

"Are there private ones?"

"Sure. Not actual airports, but lots of ranchers have their own landing strips right on their property."

"Do you see small planes like ones that could land on a grass runway around here often?"

"Often enough that it isn't a surprise, but not every day. Why you askin'?"

Dirk shrugged one shoulder. "I just saw a small plane flying real low earlier today. I wondered where he was going to set down. I thought maybe he was crop dusting, or something."

"Maybe. I sure couldn't say. I'll be right out with your meals."

Hank sucked in a slug of his Juicy Haze IPA like it was a lifeline. "God, that's good."

"Needed a drink, huh?"

"You're telling me? I've been on rations lately—special diet and all."

"Why?"

Hank's neck grew splotchy, and he stared into his glass. "Certain foods, and no alcohol are supposed to speed up the swimmers."

Dirk considered Hank for a minute. "So, why the beer?"

"Sometimes I need a break. I need my life back."

"You know, kid, I don't know much, but if you aren't into this fertility thing, you need to be honest with Amy. You'll end up resenting the whole process—maybe even your wife. You're already sneaking around."

"Yeah, well, one beer isn't going to kill me, and I won't see Amy 'til tomorrow. This will be out of my system by then." Hank chugged half the pint.

Dirk kept his own counsel. None of this was his business, and he sure as hell wasn't about to judge. "I noticed tire tracks back inside the Quonset hut, obviously made by a huge truck. And at the back door there were two thin tire tracks running parallel with a smaller one in the middle. That's the kind of print a small airplane would make."

"You think someone's using the place as a hangar or maybe a point of transfer?"

"Probably, but that alone isn't illegal."

"Maybe Crandall has set up business there."

"It's possible, but we have no evidence of that other than a bloody note attached to a dead man's head. So far, it's just a coincidence of MO that connects Crandall to all of this, and that's pretty thin."

Juanita returned with a plate-sized smothered burrito for Dirk and a cheeseburger for Hank. Dirk thanked her and said, "I bet you see everyone around here within the space of a month or so."

"Probably within a week." She laughed.

He held up a photo on his phone "Have you ever seen this guy in town?"

She stared at his screen but gave no reaction. "You guys cops or something?"

"Or something. We were tasked with informing him of some sad personal news, but we can't seem to find him."

"What kind of news?"

"The deceased family member kind."

"That's awful. I can't imagine having some strangers show up to tell me somebody I loved was dead."

"It's no fun being the bearer of sad news either."

"I bet." Juanita stood at the edge of their table deep in thought—no doubt imagining herself in such a scenario.

"So, have you ever seen him?"

She blinked and came back to the present. "Oh. Sorry. No, I haven't. Want me to ask around at the bar?"

Dirk considered it but didn't want to tip his hand that they were hunting Crandall. It was always easier to find your prey when they didn't smell you coming. "No, thanks. If you haven't seen him, I don't suppose anyone has. Thanks, though."

After dinner, he and Hank walked back to the small inn. The owner was still sitting behind the check-in desk. "Did you boys have a nice supper?"

"You always find the best food is in small towns," Hank answered, and the man smiled with pride.

Dirk leaned against the desk and held up Crandall's mugshot. "Have you ever seen this guy come through here?"

The older man took Dirk's phone out of his hand and held it close to his face. "No, can't say I have. But lots of folks come through here, you know?"

"Yeah, I suppose. Tell me, how much airplane traffic do you see on a day-to-day basis?"

"Plenty. Unfortunately, it rarely turns into business for me. I'm not sure why folks land here if they don't want to stay and look around."

"Maybe they're refueling or practicing touch-and-goes."

"I suppose. That's about how long a plane stays here before it takes off, that's for sure. Me and my Eleanor used to enjoy sitting on our back porch on my days off and watching the planes come and go."

Hank, looking at personal photos hung on the wall behind the desk, asked, "Is this Eleanor?"

"Yes. That was a marvelous day. Look how happy she is. She won a blue ribbon for her huckleberry pie at the county fair that day." A wistfulness filled the man's eyes and voice. "She passed four years ago."

"I'm sorry." Compassion filled Hank's expression. "I can see you loved her very much."

"That's true. Now, I'm just filling days."

Dirk stepped in. "I wonder if you'd mind doing us a favor?"

"Depends on what it is."

"We're interested in how many planes fly in and out of Johnson County. Would you mind counting the ones you see over the next week and letting us know what you find?"

The bent man straightened. "Sure. That's a favor I'd love to do for you. Do you want to know what kinds of planes they are, too?"

Surprised, Dirk gave half a grin. "You know airplanes that well?"

"I sure do. It's been a hobby of mine since I was a boy. I used to keep a log of all the planes and their tail numbers, too, back when I could see them."

"Would you mind tracking times and dates, as well?"

"Not at all."

"Well, looks like we're asking you to do something you already enjoy doing. We'll be in touch in a week or two to see what you've recorded."

"Sounds like a plan. You gents have a good night, then. I'll see you in the morning."

Dirk jotted down his name and cell number on a desk pad and he and Hank went to their rooms. They each unlocked their doors and pushed them open, but Dirk paused. "Hey, kid."

Hank stepped back out of his room. "Yeah?"

"I have one thing that needs saying."

"Okay?" Hank's brow dipped in concern.

"You need to be there for Amy. Support her and be open with her…" He swallowed against the sharp grit that suddenly clogged his throat. "Or she'll find someone else who will." Without waiting for Hank to respond, he went into his room and closed the door.

CHAPTER 4

The man's whimpering chewed on Beaux's last nerve. He glared over the front seat of the old Monte Carlo at the man sniveling in the backseat. "Shut up you moron. You're the one who was running your mouth at the bar. You're the only one to blame for the situation you're in."

"I didn't! It wasn't me!" the man wailed.

"Shut your suck, or I'll pull over and do it for you." Troy drove their captive's car deep into the dark Montana night along a road people rarely used. Beaux's second bodyguard, Rufus, followed them in Beaux's sleek black Cadillac CT5-V.

"I'm trying to tell you. I didn't say nothin' to nobody!" the man cried through his bloodied mouth. He spit part of a broken tooth onto the floor.

"You wear my ink mark as my employee, but you forgot what it meant. I expect blind loyalty. You failed."

"No! I—"

"Pull over and take him outside. Work him over until he confesses his guilt."

Troy nodded and stopped the car. He yanked the already abused man out of the backseat and tossed him onto the side of the dark, abandoned road. Swinging his leg back, Troy kicked him hard in the ribs with his steel-toed boots. And again, in the groin. "You gonna confess?"

The man groaned and vomited the contents of his stomach. Rufus pulled up behind the Monte Carlo and joined Troy standing over their victim. Dropping his weight onto the guy's back, Rufus cracked the traitor's spine with his knee, and forced his face into the slimy vomit.

"My partner asked you a question." Rufus lifted the man by his hair like a rag doll and held him on his feet while Troy took punching-bag practice with his face. Blood and broken teeth sprayed everywhere.

Beaux leaned against the big car watching—amazed at how much punishment the man took before he finally passed out. When the bloody face flopped forward, Beaux stood. "That's good enough. Lie him on his back and bring me the hammer."

Troy left Rufus to arrange the man's body and jogged to the Caddy for the toolbox. By the time his guard returned, Beaux had finished penning his note. He had to get his point across. What was it these people didn't understand? Beaux was taking over the local syndicate and building an empire. It was crucial that people learned to fear him.

Troy appeared at his side with the requested tool, and Beaux removed a four-inch nail from his front shirt pocket. He ran the thin shaft over his lips, savoring the moment.

Kneeling, he spread his note over the man's battered forehead. The tip of the nail held the paper in place as he raised the hammer in his other hand and swung. The man's eyes opened as the hammer fell. The terror swimming in his victim's eyes and the loud crack that followed, warmed Beaux's soul and would populate his fantasies, strengthening him in the days to come. In that moment, Beaux knew the power over life and death, and it was euphoric.

Once the nail split the weasel's skull and the note was fastened in place, Beaux dipped his fingers into the man's blood. Laughing, he smeared warrior stripes on his cheeks. "Get him back inside the Monte Carlo and drive him to the cliff. Dump him over, then ditch the car. And be quick about it. There's an iced bottle of Dom Pérignon at home waiting to be opened."

CHAPTER 5

Dirk and Hank met Sheriff Murdoch on the sidewalk in front of his office the next day. "Good morning, fellas. Come on in."

Murdoch was friendlier than he had been the previous evening. Perhaps he'd looked into the marshal's credentials and decided they were brother lawmen after all. They followed Murdoch into a large room through an office that held three desks. The office was lit with sunlight streaming through two picture windows that framed either side of the front door. They probably once served as display casements for a local shop before the space was converted into the town jail.

The sheriff introduced them to Deputy Pringle who answered phone calls and performed general administrative work. "My other deputy is off today, so I'm on duty. It's just the three of us." Murdoch rested his hands on his hips. "So, how can we help you?"

"We'd like to have a look at your investigation reports

on the murder at the Quonset hut. Do you have a copy of the ME's report?"

"The local doc plays the role of both coroner and medical examiner in this county. I can give him a call and see if he'll rush over his findings."

Dirk clapped the man's soft shoulder. "We'd sure appreciate it."

The deputy placed the requested files and a three-ring binder on top of a long table pushed against the wall of the large room, then dragged over two chairs. "You guys want some coffee, or something?"

Hank perked up. "That'd be great. Thanks."

Picking up the notebook, Dirk asked, "Is this your murder book?"

"Yeah, such as it is." Pringle filled a glass pot with cold water from a sink that was set in a counter along the same wall as the table. "We don't know much. Doesn't look like the victim was a local."

"Did you run his fingerprints through IAFIS?"

"I was going to do that this afternoon. We figured there wasn't any rush since no one around here had been reported as missing."

"Well, he had to come from somewhere, and knowing who he was and where he came from is integral to any investigation." Hank took a cup from a shelf over the sink. He held it up toward Dirk in question. He shook his head, no, and Hank repeated the gesture to the deputy and sheriff. Only the deputy nodded, and Hank pulled down another mug. "Besides, don't you think the deceased's next of kin might want to know?"

"To be honest," Pringle said as he counted out scoops of coffee and dumped them into the filter. He glanced over his shoulder at Dirk and the sheriff. He lowered his voice, though they could all still hear him. "I'm not real familiar with how the website works. I was waiting for our other deputy to show me how when he comes in for his shift tomorrow."

Murdoch raised his hands at his sides. "For cripe's sake, Pringle. If you don't know something, you gotta ask." He turned to Dirk with an apologetic grimace. "We'll run those prints right away."

"That'd be great." Dirk held onto a mild expression that didn't convey his frustration at the lack of police work they'd done.

He and Hank spent the morning poring over the case documents and photos while the sheriff taught Pringle how to use the IAFIS database. Around 11:30am, the town doctor arrived at the Sheriff's Office with his report. Dirk smirked internally, wondering why the man didn't simply email the document. But this was a tiny rural town. Lots of people probably did things the old-fashioned way.

Murdoch introduced the doctor to Dirk, and they shook hands. "Not much to go on, I'm afraid. You'll see that my investigation notes are straightforward. The victim was approximately fifty to sixty years of age and was of Hispanic descent. He died from multiple gunshot wounds to his torso. Whoever hammered the nail into his skull did it post-mortem. He'd been dead less than an hour before Deputy Pringle found him. There was no foreign tissue under his fingernails. Other than that, I can surmise by the contents of his stomach and its lining that he was a heavy drinker, and he'd ruined his lungs with continual smoking. Nutrition was not high on his list of concerns, either. His teeth had rarely seen a toothbrush, let alone a dentist. I sent his clothing to the Wyoming Crime Lab. You'll have to get their report from them."

"And the rounds? Were there any bullets left inside the body?"

"Yes. Four. The wound on his shoulder went clear through."

"I presume you sent the bullets to the crime lab along with the clothing?"

"Indeed."

Dirk canted his head toward Murdoch. "Were any rounds discovered at the scene?"

The sheriff's face paled. "No. But Pringle will go out there this afternoon with a magnetic pickup and do another search."

Dirk bit back a derogatory comment and continued to question the doctor. "Any discernible scars, tattoos, or other identifying marks?" He scanned through the doctor's official report.

"The victim had an old scar on his chin, like many of us do after weathering childhood. There was a small marijuana-leaf tattoo on the back of his neck that was approximately one inch in diameter. Nothing beyond that."

"Thanks, Doc." Dirk called over to Pringle, "How are those prints coming?"

"Nothin' so far."

"Hank, will you continue the print search with Sheriff Murdoch and let me know if you guys find anything? Pringle, I want you to take me through the photos in your file. Tell me about each image."

"You got it." Hank pulled a chair up next to the sheriff and sped up the search.

Just after noon, Hank got up from his chair. "His prints aren't in the system, Dirk."

"Huh. That's surprising. Criminals rarely get to the ripe age of fifty without doing some sort of jail time." Dirk rubbed his chin. "Pringle, talk us through everything you observed on the day of the murder. You said you saw a car driving away from the Quonset hut when you arrived."

"Yeah. It's why I got out to look around in the first place. The car I saw was black and super nice, nothing like you'd see around here."

"Did you get the make and model, or a license plate number?"

"It was too far away to tell."

"Okay, so you got out of your squad car, and then what?"

"I called out to see if anyone was there. No one answered. That's when I saw what looked like blood on the dirt and drag marks made from what I figured was the heels of boots."

"So, you followed the marks?"

"Yep. Straight in through the door to a big crate. I figured the spilled blood gave me probable cause, so I found a crowbar and opened the wooden box. There, inside, was the dead guy with his eyes wide open and a note nailed to his head." Pringle shuddered. "Everything is in my report."

"Thanks, Deputy. You did a good job." After Pringle gave his account, Dirk called the Wyoming State Crime Lab, though he had little hope they had looked at the clothing yet. State labs were always backed up. He had guessed right and was told it could be at least a week or more before they got to their particular evidence.

Dirk's phone buzzed with a call from Emory. "Hey, Chief. Sorry, I haven't checked in. We've been at the local sheriff's all morning going over their notes on the case."

"What did you find?"

"Nothing more than we already knew. I have some suspicions, but they don't come with evidence, yet. They're just dots that need connecting. I'll email the ME report to you and update the electronic casefile. Then, we'll be heading back to Montana in about an hour."

"Fine. By the way, your friend, Laurie called."

"Oh, crap. She probably tried to get ahold of me when I was out of cell range. Everything okay?"

"She didn't say. Just asked me to tell you she called."

"Thanks."

"Also, Ceylon Rahip tried to reach you. This isn't a dating service, you know." Emory teased but her laugh sounded forced.

"I guess it's a good thing I'm not dating either of those women, then. Was Ceylon calling on official business?"

"I don't think so, why?"

"She has my personal cell number. I wonder why she called the office?"

"I'm sure I don't know," she replied with a crisp tone. "Perhaps you were out of cell range for her call too."

"Look, Emory, you sound kind of pissed, and I get it. I don't usually take personal calls at the office. But why are *you* answering the phone? Where's Teresa?"

"Teresa is on a long lunch. There's an art show at her son's school and she went to see his painting. And I'm not pissed. Why would I be?"

"There is *surely* no reason I can think of." Her groan on

the other end of the call made him smirk. "We'll see you this afternoon."

"Wait. How's Henry?"

"Fine. And for any more than that, you'll have to talk directly with him. See you soon."

"Drive safe."

"Will do."

On their way back to Billings, Dirk returned his messages. First, he dialed Ceylon. Hers would be the easiest call to deal with. "Hey, Ceylon. It's Dirk Sterling. How are you liking New York City?"

"Hello, Dirk. Thank you for returning my phone call. New York is exciting, but I am not currently there."

"No? Where are you?"

"I've been traveling around the United States, this summer. It is a vast country."

"It is that. Where all have you gone?"

"I went to the bomb site in San Francisco, hoping to make amends and bring peace."

Dirk chewed on his bottom lip. Ceylon's father was responsible for a bombing in the city that took place a couple of months ago. Her reception there could have been a disaster. "How did that go? Did you have any security?"

"No. I went on my own. For the most part, I think the people I spoke with felt like they were not forgotten. Others were understandably angry."

"Maybe it was too soon."

"Yes, you are probably right. From there I traveled east, through Moab and into Colorado."

"Where are you now?"

"That's why I'm calling. I'm still in Colorado, and when I looked at the map, I realized I'm only two states away from you. Would it be fine if I came to visit you in Montana? You said you had a cabin?"

"Of course, and you're welcome anytime. But you should know that those two states are big, and it'll take you a full day to drive up here."

"I did not realize. Everything is so big here. Is it still okay?"

"Absolutely. It will give my housekeeper some time to get to the cabin clean, and make sure the linens are fresh."

"Please don't go to any trouble. I just thought it would be a nice break before I start university in September."

"It's no trouble at all. Why don't you call me when you cross the Montana border and I'll give you directions from there."

"Maybe I should spend the day in Denver, turn in my rental car, and fly up to Billings."

"Perfect, I'll pick you up at the airport, then."

"Thank you. I'm excited to see the beautiful state where you live."

"It will be nice to see you again."

Ceylon's voice softened. "You too," she said before ending the call.

Hank watched him from the corner of his eye. "Ceylon's coming to Billings?"

"Yeah. She's going to stay up at my cabin in the Bear Mountains for a few days before she goes to college."

"Good for her."

"She's an amazing young woman. Brave. She'll make a good doctor." Dirk thought about the women in his life and wondered if he could clear up all the personal messes he'd made in one big sweep. "I think I'll throw a dinner party for Ceylon when she gets here. What do you think? Would you and Amy come?"

"Depends on her temperature." Hank rolled his eyes.

"You could always stay overnight. There's plenty of room."

"I'll ask her."

"Good. I'll invite the chief and Aldrich, too. And Laurie and Caleb. Get the whole gang together."

Hank's lips twitched like he wanted to laugh but decided against it.

"What?"

"Nothing." Hank did laugh then. "Just sounds like a big bowl of trouble to me. That's all."

"What do you mean?"

"You want to have a dinner party with three women— all who have a thing for you—all at one time? Are you crazy?"

"What are you talking about?" Dirk crunched his brows together. "Ceylon doesn't have a thing for me, and neither does the chief. She's seeing Aldrich. And Laurie… well, that's complicated. I'm working on that."

"Right. Dream on, Sterling. Ceylon suffers from idol worship. And I understand that whatever is going on between you and Dillinger's family is multi-layered. But Grey? The tension between you two at the office is hard to walk through. It's a tangible thing, like being waist deep in the Goop kids play with. Ask Teresa."

Dirk glared at Hank. "You and Teresa talk about Emory and me?"

"No. Not talk, exactly. It's more like throwing each

other life preservers when you two are splashing around in your sea of innuendos."

"Shut up, kid. You don't know what you're talking about. I was thinking it would be an opportunity for the chief to see there is nothing but friendship between me and Laurie. And Laurie could see the same thing between me and Emory. I'm tired of trying to convince them about each other."

"Sounds to me more like you're trying to convince yourself."

"Didn't I tell you to shut up? Pay attention to the road," Dirk groused, and Hank laughed as he shifted his gaze forward and pressed the accelerator.

CHAPTER 6

Emory smoothed her hair and straightened her blazer before stepping out of her office to greet Dirk and Henry when they returned that afternoon. "Welcome back." She kept her gaze focused on Henry rather than directly meeting Dirk's eyes. "Why don't you guys take five to get settled? Then, meet me in the conference room for a debrief."

"Yes, ma'am." Dirk shrugged out of his leather jacket and tossed it on the back of his chair. He leaned against the edge of his desk. "Hey, Mendez, how was the art show? You got a Michael Angelo on your hands?"

"*I* certainly think so." Teresa grinned and held up her phone with a photo of her son's painting for Dirk to see.

"Well, I'm no art-major, but that looks like quality work to me." He winked at her. "I'm gonna grab a bottle of water. Either of you want anything?"

"I'll take one, too. Thanks." Henry relaxed into his desk chair. "I want to call Amy quick before the meeting."

"Good idea. I'll meet you in there."

For the next hour, Dirk and Henry rehashed the events of the previous night and that morning for Emory's benefit. They gave her a thorough report, but all it told her was that they had almost nothing to go on. "Well, I guess we keep digging. Dirk, is the Wyoming Crime Lab going to let you know if they find anything?"

"Yes, they'll call me right after they talk to the local Sheriff's Office."

"Good work, guys. Let's see what we can find out about our mystery dead man. It makes no sense that there isn't a record of him. Hopefully, we'll learn his identity soon." Emory tapped her pen on the tabletop. "I've been in touch with the Chief Deputies in Cody, Wyoming, and Rapid City, South Dakota. I wanted them all to be on alert for the killer as well, so I shared our files on the John Doe in Wyoming and sent them the ME's report. I gave them everything we have on Crandall, too. Just in case he and the murderer are the same man. I also touched base with the Reservation Police over at Crow Agency."

Dirk nodded. "Good thinking. We'll find the guy, Chief. Count on it."

"I do." Her phone vibrated against her hip from inside her blazer pocket. "Excuse, me." She answered the call swiveling her chair so that her back was to her deputies. "This is Chief Grey."

"Chief, this is Captain Strongbow. After you called this morning, one of my officers reported finding a dead body near Yellowtail, by the river."

"I'm sorry to hear that, Captain. Do you think the body has something to do with our case? There's no note attached to the body's forehead, is there?"

The native police captain snorted. "No, but there is a

tattoo of a Maryjane leaf on the back of his neck. Just thought you might want to know."

"Yes, thank you. Do you mind if I send some deputies down there this afternoon to check it out?"

"Fine with me."

"Great. Thanks for the call, Captain." Emory turned her chair to face the conference table, again. "That was the Police Captain at Crow Agency. One of his officers found a dead body with a marijuana leaf tattoo."

"We heard your side of the conversation." Dirk sat forward. "Do you want me and Hank to go down there?"

Henry dropped his chin and released a long breath. Dirk studied Henry for a few seconds before he shifted his stormy eyes to her. "I can go on my own. It doesn't sound like a job for two. I'll just be looking at a dead guy and talking to Captain Strongbow. Besides, Hank deserves to get off on time, for once." The look Dirk gave her reached deep inside and was heavy with meaning. The guys must have talked while they were on their road trip.

"I agree. If you don't mind going on your own, that makes the most sense."

"No problem. I've got my hog, and it will be a nice drive." By hog, Dirk referred to the Bonneville T120 Motorcycle he loved to ride. Emory's thoughts drifted into a daydream about riding on the back of his bike and going off on a long weekend getaway with him. A smile softened her mouth.

"Chief?"

"Oh." She snapped her attention back to the room. "Sorry, my mind strayed there for a minute." Her face filled with heat, and she gathered her papers and iPad.

"That's good. Fine. Report back and let me know if you discover any connections to our case."

"I *surely* will." His eyes glinted with humor. The man was relentless with his teasing.

"Good. That'll be all. Henry, why don't you take the rest of the day off."

"Thanks, Chief. That'd be awesome!" Henry jumped to his feet, nodded at Dirk, and left the room. Dirk continued to lean back in his chair assessing her with an insolent grin.

"You'd better get going, Sterling."

"I will, but before I go, I wanted to tell you that Ceylon Rahip is coming into town for a couple of days. She'll be staying at my cabin."

"Oh?" Emory dropped her pen. Dirk leaned down to pick it up for her and they bumped heads. "I'm sorry," she whispered. He was too close. She rubbed the sore spot on her temple.

"Not a problem." He returned to his chair. "You okay?"

"Fine." Emory's heart ping-ponged against her ribs and she cleared her throat. "I didn't realize you and Ceylon were that close."

"Close?" His brows dipped and then his eyes opened wide. "Oh—no—it's not like that. I'll be at my house in Billings. She just needs a place to chill for a little while before she starts school, and I offered my cabin. Anyway, I thought it would be good if we had a welcome dinner for her. You could bring Aldrich, if you want."

"Oh." Dirk seemed completely comfortable with that idea which surprised her. "Okay. When are you thinking?"

"Next weekend. Hank and Amy are probably coming,

but I still need to ask Teresa and Laurie. It will be nice to get everyone together, don't you think?"

For half a second, Emory thought she saw a boy's earnestness in his eyes, but it quickly vanished—replaced by the devil-may-care attitude he generally cloaked himself with.

"Yes, I think that's very thoughtful. Let me know what you'd like me to bring."

"Nothing. I got it covered."

Hm. This she had to see. "Okay. I'll ask Dave if he can come, and I'll let you know."

Dirk grabbed his jacket and after sending a teasing jab in Henry's direction, he stopped to invite Teresa and her little boy to his dinner party. Then he was out the door. Emory watched him from her office window as he fitted his sleek helmet over his head and swung his leg over the saddle of the motorcycle. She felt the deep rumble of the engine clear up inside the building when he kick-started the bike. *God, that man should be in a motorcycle commercial.*

Emory shook her head to stop her wanton thoughts from following Dirk down the road. She tapped Dave's number into her phone.

"Hello, beautiful."

"Hi, Dave. What are you doing next weekend?"

"Why Chief Grey, are you asking me out on a date?"

She smiled. "Yes, I am. Dirk is holding a dinner party up at his cabin in the Bear Mountains in honor of Ceylon Rahip who is coming to Montana for a visit, and he's invited us."

"I'm sure Sterling invited you, but does he know you're including me?"

"Actually, he suggested it."

"Interesting."

"Why?"

"Nothing. I'm at your beck and call. Friday or Saturday?"

"I don't know yet. Are you flexible?"

"For you? You'd be amazed at how flexible I can be."

CHAPTER 7

irk loved riding his motorcycle on the country roads. His chest expanded with the fresh air and wide-open spaces as he raced toward the Reservation, and it didn't seem long before he glided into the gravel parking lot at the Crow Police Station. He clipped his helmet to his bike and went inside.

"Hey," he said to the receptionist as he held up his silver star. "Deputy US Marshal Sterling, looking for Captain Strongbow."

The solid woman behind the desk smiled up at him. "I'll tell him you're here."

She went down the hall to one of a series of offices. The woman returned seconds later and motioned for him to follow her. Stopping at an open doorway, she swept her hand in front of herself gesturing for him to enter the office.

"Thank you," he said. She bowed her head, silently returning to her workstation.

"Deputy Sterling," a man of proud bearing who looked

to be in his mid-fifties with long, still mostly black braids, stood from behind his desk, "I'm Thomas Strongbow. I gather you're here to check out our dead white guy."

Dirk liked the man right away and shook his hand. "Sure am."

"Follow me." Dirk walked with Strongbow outside to his captain's cruiser. "The body is over at the clinic. It's a short drive."

Dirk opened the passenger's door. "Gunshot to the head, did you say? Where was the entry point?"

The men got in and Strongbow started the engine. He backed out of his personal parking spot without answering Dirk until he pulled onto the road heading deeper into the Reservation. "Yep. They shot the poor soul right between the eyes."

"And the exit wound?"

"Wasn't one."

"Huh. Maybe a .22?"

"That was my guess too, but I'm waiting for the medical report."

"Will the doctor be at the clinic this afternoon?"

"Maybe yes, maybe no." Longbow looked out the window at the sky. "Might have gone fishing."

Dirk reminded himself it behooved him to appreciate the cultural differences between the nature-loving natives and his own fast paced, clock-oriented one. "A good day for it."

The captain snickered. "It is. You almost missed me for that same reason."

Together they entered the clinic and went down to the basement that was kept cold with air-conditioning units mounted in the small windows. Hauntingly beautiful flute music echoed from inside the morgue. Strongbow knocked on an office door directly opposite the exam room.

"Enter."

The captain opened the door and leaned in. "Hey Jimmy, will you show us the body Long Feather brought in yesterday?"

"Sure. But I've started the internal exam, so it's kind of graphic. Did you eat lunch?"

"We'll be fine." Strongbow stepped aside and introduced Dirk. The doctor shook his hand and walked across the hall to the cool room. "Right this way."

The body lay on a stainless-steel gurney and was draped from the waist down with a single sheet, folded back exposing the Y incision and open chest cavity. The victim was a white guy, though it was hard to tell by his face which was a swirl of deep reds and purples. Dirk approached the table. If he had to guess, the man had been in his mid-twenties and didn't appear to be a person who took good care of himself. His hair was long and scraggly, and his fingernails were dirty and chewed off. "Any idea who this guy was, Captain?"

"No."

Dirk studied the small hole in the center of the body's forehead and frowned. "You believe he was shot in the head?"

"That is what Sergeant Long Feather reported."

The doctor pulled on a pair of gloves and palpated the tissue around the entry hole. "But this, in fact, is not a bullet wound."

"What is it?" Dirk leaned closer.

"This hole is a puncture wound, but not one made by a

bullet. The man's cause of death was a large nail hammered into his skull, where it pierced his brain."

Dirk winced. That explained why there was no exit wound. "Are you saying he was alive when someone rammed the nail into his skull?"

The doctor's broad lips flattened into a straight line. "I'm afraid that is exactly what I'm saying."

"Have you found any trace evidence that might indicate the identity of his killer? Tissues, fibers, anything like that?"

"Not yet. The nail was removed before the sergeant found the body, which is why he assumed it was a gunshot wound. The victim suffered a harsh beating prior to death, and there are ligature marks on his wrists, indicating he was bound. But it was the nail that killed him."

"Do you think he was conscious when the hammer hit the nail?"

"Hard to say, but it was a clean blow. I suppose it is possible the man was too frightened to move."

"Maybe." Dirk considered that as he tried to imagine the scene. "Captain, did your sergeant find any handwritten notes on or around the body?"

"Nothing. Just the body."

Dirk stared at the young dead face. "Any distinguishing marks?"

"Appendectomy scar, and three small tattoos. Pictures of each are on the board."

Dirk crossed the room and studied the photos—one scar, and ink of Sonic the Hedgehog, a dagger, and a pot leaf. He pointed to the tattoo that matched the victim's ink in Wyoming "Where on the body is this tattoo located?

"Backside of the neck."

Dirk's nerves revved the way they did whenever he was on someone's trail. "Where exactly did Long Feather find this guy?"

"Well, now. That's the rub." The captain crossed his arms. "Long Feather found the body about twenty feet this side of the Res border. But he could have been killed on state land and dragged onto the Res by a wild animal." An ironic smile stirred his lips. "My report might depend on how much paperwork the location of his death entails."

Dirk shook his head and chuckled. "Will you take me to where the body was found?"

The captain looked at his watch. "I suppose I could. But it's up in the hills. Best accessed from the saddle. You any good with horses?"

"I did pretty well staying on the backs of furious bulls when I was a kid, so yeah, I can hold my own on a horse." Dirk hadn't thought of his rodeo days since the last time he was on a horse, chasing fugitives through the Wyoming mountains with Caitlyn Reed… and Sam. A brief smile moved his lips at the thought of his old partner bouncing around in the saddle like a jumping bean. Sam had been shot in the leg during that chase, but he complained more about his butt hurting from the ride.

A couple of hours later, Dirk helped Strongbow unload their horses from the trailer at the end of the mountain road. Soon he was following the captain up a rocky path through the steep crevices that overlooked a section of Big Horn Lake. "What was your sergeant doing all the way up here?"

"Hunting."

It wasn't hunting season, but Dirk supposed the laws were different on the Res. He'd leave the complex Treaty

Laws up to Fish and Game. "Did he come across the body just by chance? Was anyone else with him who can confirm his report?"

Strongbow gave him a long level look. "I don't like your implication, Deputy."

"I'm not implying anything. Just being thorough."

"Right." The captain nudged his horse into a trot, and Dirk kept pace. "He was with his son."

Eventually, they arrived at a small mountain meadow with a crystal-clear river that wound around the foot of a rocky cliff. The dead body had matted the grasses down on the bank. Strongbow dismounted at the edge of the clearing.

"Where is the Res border from here?"

"The border follows the river."

Dirk followed the river as far as his eyes could see. There were mountains on either side.

Strongbow pointed to the top of the cliff. "That, up there, is state land. There's a road on top of that cliff."

"That's sheer rock. Was the victim killed up there, or down below where Long Feather found him?"

"It's hard to say, but I think he was pushed over the edge. You saw all the bruising on the body."

"I thought that was from a beating. Do you think the murderer was purposely trying to make it look like the man was killed on Crow land?"

"Wouldn't surprise me. I doubt we'll ever know."

"Maybe." Dirk hopped down from his saddle and methodically scouted the area. Something caught in the leaves of a bush fluttered in the late afternoon sun, catching his eye. Careful not to disturb anything that might later be deemed as evidence, Dirk crouched by a scrap of white. It was a crumpled-up piece of notebook paper.

Pulling a rubber glove from a pouch he kept on his belt, he snapped it on his right hand and flattened the paper against his thigh. It was a hand-written note. *This shitty performance ends now. There's a new Chief in town. One who expects complete and utter loyalty—or a miserable death.*

CHAPTER 8

Hank clenched his jaw and buried his face in his hands—breathing deeply so he could keep his patience. He shouldn't have taken the afternoon off. He wouldn't have if he'd known he would be dealing with Amy in full-on battle mode.

He tried again, "How many times do I have to say it? We thought we'd be home last night, but things changed. Field situations are dynamic. They change all the time. And I have to be able to pivot."

"What's more important to you? Your job, or me? Me *and* our future family? Is this how it's going to be when we have kids? Come on, Hank. Just admit it. Dirk Sterling wiggles his little finger and you go running." Amy slammed a kitchen cupboard. "I wish I was only half that important to you."

He groaned. "Amy, you know you mean more to me than my job. It's not either-or, it's both-and. You are the most important thing to me, but my career is important too. And ultimately, it's how I'll provide for a family if and when we have one. I'm still a rookie at work. I need to prove my salt. Why can't you understand that?"

"Because I want to get pregnant and that's impossible to do by myself." Another cabinet door shook on its hinges. "And what do you mean 'if and when we have one?' You sound so matter of fact, like you don't care."

"Come on, Amy. That's not fair." Hank let an angry retort dissolve on his tongue and swallowed it. "One thing I know for sure, all this yelling and stress can't be good for trying to get pregnant."

"No? What do you know? You've missed the last two doctor appointments." His wife's light brown eyes flashed with anger and hurt. She was looking for a fight that he didn't want to have. But she was pushing all his buttons.

Hank realized his hands were in tight fists, so he stretched out his fingers to release the tension. "Those were *your* doctor appointments. I didn't need to be there."

"I'd have thought you would *want* to be there. But no. You'd rather race all over the countryside chasing dirtbags." She stormed down the hallway to their bedroom.

Under his breath, Hank murmured, "They're a hell of a lot easier to deal with than you."

Amy appeared at his side with tears flooding her eyes. "I heard that." How did she do that? Was she a ninja or something?

"I'm sorry, Amy. I didn't mean it. It's just that you say you want me home, but when I'm here, all we do is fight. Or you tap your watch and expect me to hop up and impregnate you on demand. Amy, this is no kind of life. Remember when it was fun to make love to each other? Can't we go back to that?"

"I remember. And now, the last thing you want is to be

with me. I also remember a time when you couldn't keep your hands off me. Have I changed so much? Don't you find me attractive anymore?"

"Of course, I do." Hank pressed his eyes closed with his thumb and middle finger. This argument was going in circles that made no sense. "It's not that. It's the being on a clock and temperature watch that sucks the desire out of it. I want to go back to being spontaneous."

"There will be plenty of time for that when I'm pregnant." Hank's phone buzzed, and Amy narrowed her eyes making him loathe to pick it up. She made a point of looking at her watch. "It's eight-thirty at night, but go ahead, answer it. I'm sure it's your hero, Dirk. No one else ever calls you." Her voice dripped with acid.

He sighed and lifted his phone. She was right, it was his partner. "Hey, Sterling. What's up."

Hank listened to Dirk's story of what he'd found on the Crow Reservation. "Holy crap. Do you think we're dealing with a serial killer? I mean we've got a repeated MO, the calling cards of the notes, and the tattoos." The idea sent a shiver of excitement through him. He'd almost applied to the FBI because he liked the idea of investigating serial murders, but something about the mission of hunting fugitives sounded a louder call to his deep sense of justice.

"I don't think that's the case here." Dirk's deep voice echoed through Hank's receiver. "I think we're dealing with a crime boss making sure everyone around knows who's in charge. Anyway, I'm calling to see if you want to come down to the pub and grab a beer with the chief, Teresa, and me. We're going over the evidence I came across today."

Hank hesitated. Hell yes, he wanted to leave his house

and get a beer with Dirk and the team. But there would be absolute hell to pay if he did. He gripped his phone hard and refused to think about the consequences. Sometimes hell was a price worth paying. "Yeah. Absolutely. I'll be there in half an hour."

Amy stood with her arms crossed and her eyes sending poisonous darts. "I suppose you're running off to be with Dirk—wagging your tail behind you."

"He's my partner, Amy. We're in the middle of an important case. The whole team is meeting. I can't be the only one who doesn't show up."

"You're always on an *important case.*" She air-quoted the words.

"If one of *your* relatives was murdered, you'd think it was the most important case in the world. The guy we're looking for is a cold-blooded killer. Would you rather I sit this one out? Let him kill again?" He sighed with his whole being. "Look, I'll be home in a couple of hours. Maybe we can start this evening over then?"

Amy shook her head. "It's too late for that." She snatched her phone off the counter and marched back toward their bedroom. "Hi, it's me. He's at it again…" The door slammed.

Hank's chest ached, and he was weary to the depth of his bones. That beer was going to taste fantastic. He grabbed his keys and left.

The team was already seated and halfway through their pints when Hank walked into the neighborhood watering hole. They'd done a decent amount of damage to a huge platter of nachos on the table before them. His partner raised his glass when he saw him, and Hank waved his hand in return.

He slid into the booth next to Chief Grey and faced Dirk. "Tell me everything."

Dirk recounted his trip to the Res. "The thing is, either the nail came out during the fall, or someone removed it and crumpled the note. I doubt whoever the message was intended for, received it."

"Two dead bodies within a week." Excitement bubbled through Hank's blood warming him and chasing away his issues at home. "I think we should leave the possibility of a serial killer open."

"I really don't think so, and here's why: Each body we've found is sending a message to someone. The first note complained of sloppy, late work. The second one of a lack of loyalty. I think we've got ourselves a burgeoning crime lord who wants to breed loyalty through fear."

"And you believe it's Beaux Crandall?" Hank scrolled to the man's photo on his phone.

"I don't know for sure, yet. The similarities in the MOs are hard to overlook, still it could be anyone with a sick sadistic mind. Besides, no one ever proved that the note-to-skull MO was Crandall's. It was just a suspicion. Either way, we've got to find this guy."

"Where is the note now?" Teresa asked.

"Tribal police have it in their evidence locker. They found the dead body in their jurisdiction. It's their case. We're just lucky they were willing to share their find with us."

Teresa pulled a long drink from her glass. "Did they call the FBI, too?"

The chief sipped her dark brew which left a thin line of foam on her upper lip. She wiped it off on the back of her hand. "Not that I know of. I think the tribal police are handling the case as an isolated murder." Grey tugged a chip dripping with cheese and salsa from the mound of nachos. "I can't wait until we hear back from the State Crime Lab, but we need to keep searching through the investigation reports. I want a list of any and all similarities in these crimes along with those that they suspected Crandall of in Louisiana."

Teresa downed the last gulp of her pale ale. "Well gang, as exciting as this case is, motherhood calls. I told the sitter I'd be home by nine-thirty. I gotta go."

Dirk slid out to let Teresa out of the booth. "Thanks for coming, T. I always appreciate your insight."

"Thank you, for the beer. It's so nice to have a few minutes of grown-up time." She laughed and waved as she left the bar. Teresa had sacrificed her active role as a deputy when her ex-husband left her and their son. She decided to become more of an office admin. It was important she always be around for her kid. Hank respected that, but did he want the same thing for himself? Honestly —No. Did that make him an ass? Maybe.

The chief was watching him with her intense green eyes. She didn't miss much. "So, Henry, how's Amy?"

"She's good."

"Was she okay with you not making it home last night and then turning around and coming out with the team, tonight?"

Hank squirmed, but Dirk stepped in deflecting Grey's inquiry. "The kid just stopped in for a quick drink and now he's outta here."

"Okay," Grey's all-knowing eyes drilled into him. "But next time we all grab a beer, bring Amy along. It'd be good for us all to get to know each other and for your wife to feel a part of things. How are you two settling into your new neighborhood?"

"Slowly." Hank did not want to talk about his home life. He came out for a beer to escape that misery and to relax. He swallowed his last gulp and was about to order a second when Dirk asked for the check.

As Dirk signed the bill, he glanced up. "Go ahead. Get outta here, kid. If I had a woman at home waiting for me, I'd have left a long time ago."

If Dirk only knew what going home was truly like for him, he wouldn't be so quick to send him back there. "I thought you said you weren't interested in long-term relationships."

"Hence, my presence at the bar." Dirk smirked.

CHAPTER 9

Emory sat at her desk writing reports defending the funds allotted to the Billings Marshals Office. She'd known that a position as Chief US Deputy Marshal meant plenty of paperwork, but she had foolishly believed she'd still occasionally get to be in the field with her team. Over the past several months, she realized that those occasions were rare. She was currently coming up with team-building events she could spend some of her budget on. One thing she knew for sure, if you didn't use it, you'd definitely lose it.

Her desk phone rang, and she picked up the receiver. "Yes?"

Teresa's strong voice forced her to yank the phone away from her ear. "Captain Strongbow is on line one."

"Thank you, Teresa." Emory pressed the flashing hold button. "Good morning, Captain. What can I do for you?"

"Good morning, Chief Grey. I'm calling to inform you that state investigators have determined the dead man we found yesterday *was* killed on state land, dragged, and then dropped over the cliff onto native land."

"How did they determine that?"

"State Patrol found an abandoned car off the highway outside of Edgar. Investigators detected blood smeared in both the driver's and the backseat that matches the victim's type."

"So, provided there's a DNA match, they think the vic was killed inside the car?"

"Hard to say. There were signs of a struggle on the side of the road near the top of the cliff close to the boundary of the Res. Could be the guy was dead before they threw him over the edge. Our doctor believes the cause of death was the nail, not the fall."

Emory shuddered at the mental image. "Has the sheriff over in Carbon County started an investigation, then?"

"I'm sure he has."

"Thanks, Captain. I'll send some deputies over to talk with the sheriff. Thank you for working with us."

Emory pushed back from her desk and walked out to the bullpen. Dirk glanced up and almost smiled before he schooled his features. "Hey Chief, what's up?" She wished he'd let himself relax. He had a great smile the rare times he allowed himself the indulgence.

"Looks like yesterday's victim was not killed on the Reservation. State Patrol found an abandoned vehicle out near Edgar with blood inside that matches the victim's type."

Hank leaned back in his chair. "That doesn't prove it was him. Or that he was killed there. It only places someone with his blood type in that car at some point."

Emory had to agree. "Hopefully, the lab can rush the

DNA testing through. Either way, there were signs of a struggle on the clifftop overlooking where they found the body."

"Yeah, someone messed the guy up pretty bad, so that assumption tracks." Dirk tapped his pen on his desk. "But the tribal doc said it was the nail that killed him, not the fall. So, I have to agree with the state cops. The note I found was crumpled and tossed away. I wonder if the receiver of the message wrenched the nail out of the guy's skull to get the note. We need to find that nail."

Emory perched on the edge of Henry's desk. "I want the two of you to go over to Carbon County and see what you can learn from the local sheriff. I'll try to put some pressure on the state investigators and the lab to get us that DNA information, ASAP."

"Sounds good." Dirk gathered his badge and wallet. "If we get out of here right now, we should be back in time for dinner."

"Don't worry about it on my account." Henry grabbed his jacket and lowered his voice though everyone in the office still heard him. "Apparently, I'm off the clock at home for a couple of weeks. Amy went to stay with her mother."

"Geo-bachelors, then. We can grab some food on our way home." Dirk rested his hand on the back of Henry's neck as they walked out the door.

"Done."

Her deputies left the office, and Emory returned to her desk to call the Montana State Crime Lab. She would have had more sway if the murder had happened on federal land, but since it seemed that was not the case, she simply asked if they would put her office on the "to be informed" list for information's sake. After all, as deputy marshals, their job was to hunt fugitives, not investigate them.

———

Dirk rode shotgun in Hank's truck while he drove west on I-90 and then south toward Red Lodge. They arrived at the Carbon County Sheriff's Office just after noon. The office was housed in a stately brick courthouse in the center of town. The partners went inside and climbed the stairs to the second floor where a receptionist told them the sheriff was out for lunch.

Dirk leaned on the counter. "Is there anyone here who can talk with us about the recent murder victim found on the Crow Reservation yesterday?"

"I don't know, but you're welcome to ask around."

The nearest deputy, a hefty man in his early thirties pushed himself out of his chair and offered his hand. "You guys are US Marshals, right? That's so cool."

"*Deputy* US Marshals," Dirk corrected and shook the man's hand. "I'm Sterling and this is Flannigan. We're here to learn all we can about the dead guy tribal police found on the Res yesterday."

"Oh, yeah. Crazy, right? A four-inch nail right in the noggin!"

Hank pulled out his phone and swiped to his notes app where he kept a list of evidence. "Did anyone ever find the nail?"

"No, not yet. But I worked in construction for years. The killer used a four-inch fastener nail. No other nail would have made a hole with that diameter."

"That's good insight. What else do you know about the victim?"

"Not much. We still haven't ID him. Why'd they bring you guys in on the case?"

Dirk pointed to some chairs against the wall. "Mind if we sit?"

"No, please, let me." The deputy hurried to get them seats. He dragged two spare folding chairs over and set them up next to his desk.

"Thanks." Dirk sat and leaned forward bracing himself on his knees. "We're interested in the man who killed the victim. We think he's a wanted fugitive."

Hank pulled Crandall's photo up on his phone. "Have you ever seen this man around here anywhere?"

The deputy peered at the image of the full face on the screen and shook his head. "Can't say I have." He took the phone and showed it to the other deputy who shrugged and shook his head, no.

"You might try Bella over at the dine," the receptionist offered. "She notices every new face that comes through town, and she'd know if that man was here recently."

"Good thinking. I'm hungry for lunch, anyway." Dirk pressed a hand against his belly. "Anywhere else we should ask around?"

"What exactly are you asking around about?" A nasally voice came from behind them. He addressed Hank but the kid deferred to him.

"Sheriff Donnelly?" Dirk reached out his hand, but the sheriff did not return the gesture.

"That's me, and I can't say as I appreciate you poking your nose into things around here. This isn't a federal case."

"No, you're right. But a fugitive we're looking for might be linked with your case. We were hoping we could work together."

"Leave your card with the receptionist, and I'll be in touch if we come across anything that could help you."

Dirk didn't appreciate the brush-off, but he slid a card from his wallet and handed it to the admin. "We'll be over at the diner grabbing lunch if you think of anything. That's my cell number."

Dirk thanked the deputy who had been helpful and left, followed by Hank.

They drove through town looking for the local diner. It was a classic 1950s building with the vintage signage still intact. The front and sides were all glass, and the roof slanted at a jaunty angle. "I hope the food here is as good as I remember it being in places like this." Dirk hopped out of the truck and led the way across the parking lot.

Inside the restaurant was a long counter complete with a glass-domed tray of doughnuts. Chrome and red-vinyl stools stood in front. At the end of the counter, was a circular glass cabinet with three revolving shelves holding pie slices. The servers wore gold uniform dresses with white aprons. The diner reminded Dirk of the Azar's Big Boy his parents used to take him to when he was a kid. A wave of nostalgia flowed through him. He hadn't thought of his parents in a long time.

"This place reminds me of something you'd see in those old black-and-white movies." Hank laughed.

"Hey, now. I'd have thought you were too young to have ever seen a black-and-white film."

"Touché."

A server approached them and asked how many. She selected two menus and told them to follow her.

"Do you mind if we sit on the far end of the counter?" Dirk determined it was the best location to observe the entrance and all the other people in the restaurant.

He and Hank looked over their menus. Dirk couldn't resist the home-sick sensation of sentimentality, and he ordered a Patty-melt with fries and chocolate milk.

"Chocolate milk?" Hank snickered.

"It's what I always ordered when I was a kid. Just reliving old memories."

When their meal came, Dirk breathed in the heavy scent of the fried food, the smell rocketing him back thirty years. Halfway through their lunch, Dirk showed their server a picture of Crandall and asked if she'd ever seen him before. The woman slid her order book into the pocket of her apron and took his phone to study the photo up close. She moved her fingers over his screen to enlarge the image.

"I don't believe I've seen him before. But I could be wrong. We get a lot of people coming through here on a given day."

Hank asked if it would be alright to ask the other employees.

"Sure," the woman responded, and she walked with him to talk with each one.

A second server sauntered over to Dirk's table. "Are you guys undercover cops, or the FBI?"

"Neither."

"Why are you looking for that man? What did he do?"

"Just trying to find a friend. I'd heard he'd come through here recently."

The cook stuck his head through the kitchen pass-through window. "Let me see your guy." When Hank held up the photo, he shook his head. "Nope, I ain't seen him, neither."

Dirk drained his chocolate milk, which was too sweet, and asked their server for the check. "Is there anywhere else we might go that someone passing through town would likely stop in?"

"You mean like the biker bar in Edgar?"

"Sure, I guess. Do visitors frequently go there?"

"Oh, yeah. It's the only bar in town and it's on the Chamber of Commerce website. We get lots of out-of-towners who come through here headed for Sturgis, this time of year."

Dirk paid the bill and left a generous tip for his trip down memory lane. "Good work, kid. Let's go grab a beer."

On the way to the car, Dirk's phone buzzed with a text from Laurie. **R U any good with hot water heaters?**

Why? He wondered how old the thing was. Sam and Laurie bought the house the year Sam graduated from the academy, but he had no idea how old the place was.

No hot water.

Did U chk the pilot light?

The what?

Dirk chuckled. **I'll be over after work.**

Thx. 🤍

In the car on the way to the bar, Hank turned off the radio. "We're not really going to have a beer while we're on duty, right?"

"We're going to order one. If we show up and order a

Coke, or iced tea, or something, the locals will know we're the law and nobody will tell us anything."

Hog Heaven was a stereo-typical biker bar. A row of motorcycles stood side-by-side outside the front door, their chrome shining in the sun. Inside, the building was dark, cool, and smelled like beer. All eyes were on them as they walked across the cement floor to the bar.

The bartender was a woman in her late forties who looked like she'd lived a hard life. She had drugstore red hair and wore heavy black eyeliner on her leathery eyelids. "What can I get you boys?"

Dirk slid onto a stool. "What do you have on tap?"

"Bud, Bud-light."

"Got any Banquet?"

"In bottles."

"I'll have that."

She turned to Hank. "How about you, sweetheart? Are you even old enough to drink?" She laughed a smoker's rasp.

Hank grinned at her. "I'll have the same as my pal here. Thanks."

She left and returned with two opened bottles of beer. "Ain't seen you two 'round here before. Where you from?"

"Billings." It was always best to tell as much of the truth as possible when you were making up a cover. It was easier to remember that way.

"Not too far away, then." She wiped the already clean counter with a damp rag. "What brings you out this way?"

"We're trying to find an old neighbor of ours."

"You think he lives here in Edgar?"

"Maybe. I'm not sure if he put down roots here or not.

What's your name, darlin'?" Dirk rotated the cold bottle on the bar.

The wiry woman smiled, displaying nicotine-stained teeth. She swiped a lock of hair behind her ear and leaned close. "Molly. And yours?"

"I'm Dirk, and this is my buddy, Hank." Dirk tapped the phone Hank had set face down on the counter. "Show Molly the picture of the guy we're looking for. Maybe she's seen him around."

Hank found the photo and held it up for her. "Well, strangle the chicken and call me for dinner. I know that man. That's Johnny."

Dirk's heart kicked its pulse up a notch. "Does he live around here?"

"Not in town. He has a ranch somewhere out in the country. I'm not sure where. Why are you looking for him? Are you fellas all friends?"

"Great! He won a sweepstakes and we've been trying to find him to let him know. Are you and Johnny friends?"

"I'd say we're a little more than that."

"Oh? Well don't tell him about the sweepstakes. We want it to be a surprise. By the way, how do *you* know him?"

"I'm sleeping with him."

CHAPTER 10

Hank rolled over in the pre-dawn hours, his hand naturally stretching to find Amy, only to clutch cold sheets and her unmistakable absence. He groaned aloud attempting to dislodge the sharp rock that took up residence on his chest. For half a second, he'd lived in the dreamland of normalcy where everything was fine between him and his wife. Reality was a bleak empty bed tossed in his sleepy face.

Amy had refused to answer his phone calls up to this point, but he'd try her again as soon as he got out of the shower. His leaden heart tugged at his ribs as he turned on the hot water. He hadn't wanted her to leave. Never wanted to feel so miserable and lonely. Why had he made such a big deal out of being on call for sex? He had been such a jerk.

The steamy shower eased the acute angles of the ache in his throat. So, what if Amy wanted a baby more than she wanted him? *Shit!* The thought drew him up short. Is that how he really felt? Is that why he was resisting Amy's push to get pregnant? Was he jealous of a baby? *Their* baby, who wasn't even conceived yet? He really was an ass.

Hank swung the temperature on the lever to cold, and painful darts of water hit him in the face and chest. After a minute of icy truth, he dried off, dressed, and searched for his phone. He dialed his wife for the hundredth time. And just as many times, his call was sent to voicemail.

"Amy, please call me back. I owe you an apology, and I'd like to say it to you, not the recorder. I have to leave in a few minutes for work, so I hope you get this and call right back. I love you."

In the kitchen, he burned his toast and spilled coffee on his shirt. It was already turning out to be a truly crappy day, and it was only seven-thirty. He ran to change, knowing his carelessness would also make him late to the office. On his way out of the apartment, he grabbed his badge, gun, phone, and wallet, and jogged to his truck.

When he got to work, the chief was in her office, and Dirk was on the phone. Hank slumped into his chair, tossing his phone onto the desk. A missed-call notification lit up on the screen. He looked closer and saw, "Missed Call from Amy."

He bolted out of the chair, grasping his cell, and hurried to the break room for privacy. How had he missed her call? It had to have been when he went to change clothes. *Damn it!* He returned Amy's call, ready to grovel, but he ended up in voicemail once more. She probably thought he'd ghosted her in favor of work—again.

"Amy, I'm sorry I missed your call. Please, try again. I miss you."

———

Dirk had arrived at the office early, excited to tell Emory they had a positive ID on Beaux Crandall. They couldn't prove he was involved with the two recent murders, but that was the job of the police. Dirk knew Crandall was back in the country, starting up his life in the states somewhere near Edgar, Montana. He was a fugitive, and they would catch him.

"Emory!" He burst into her office. "Did you hear?"

"Hear what? You look awfully excited." Her green eyes lit up, sparking gold flecks he hadn't noticed before.

"I am. Yesterday, Hank and I showed Crandall's photo to a bartender over in Edgar who said she knew him. But she thinks his name is Johnny and get this—they're in an intimate relationship."

"So, not Beaux, but Johnny?" A skeptical shadow slid across her eyes.

"Yeah, but you wouldn't expect him to use his real name, would you?"

"No, but—"

"It proves Crandall is in the US. Now we just need to follow Molly—that's the bartender's name—and grab him!"

"Sounds easy." Her tone implied anything but.

"It won't be easy because we don't want to tip our hand or put Molly in any danger. Crandall probably already knows by now that two strange men were in town looking for him."

"How did you explain having a photo of her boyfriend?"

"I told her he won a sweepstake and not to say anything to him so that when we make the announcement, it will be a surprise."

"And she bought that?"

Dirk grinned. "She's excited to be part of the reveal."

Emory smiled and shook her head. "Good thinking. I can't believe she fell for it. What's your next step?"

"Definitely a stakeout, but maybe you and Teresa could do it. No one has seen either of you."

"That could be fun."

"Fun? Stakeouts are rarely fun unless the target sees you and runs and you have to chase him down. *Then*, it's fun."

"Well, it's got to be more interesting than the paperwork that I'm drowning in." Emory gestured at the papers covering her desk and grimaced. "Hey, by the way, I want to RSVP for your dinner party before I forget. Dave and I will be there."

"Great." His tone flattened with his mood.

"Dirk?" Emory's dark-blonde brows pinched together in concern.

"I mean, *great!* That's fantastic. I've got to get to the store." He forced a laugh as he left her office and went to his desk. The only people who hadn't responded to his barbeque invitation yet were Hank and Amy, and he didn't want to ask.

His phone rang. "Laurie, hi. How's it going?"

"Good. I wanted to thank you again for stopping by last night to fix my water heater."

"Not a problem. The pilot light was blown out. That's all."

"Well, I appreciate it." He heard the smile in her voice, and it brought a responding one to his lips. "What can I bring to dinner on Saturday? I could bring dessert or something."

"Nothing. I've got it all covered." Dirk nodded to Hank as he arrived at work. The kid looked rough. He had dark smudges under his eyes like he hadn't slept.

"Okay, if you say so. Let me know if you change your mind. By the way, Caleb will be staying overnight with my mom that night."

"He doesn't have to, you know. I'd love to see him, and he'd have his own room to spend the night in."

"That's sweet, but I already have the overnight with Grandma arranged. She's keeping him for the whole weekend."

"That sounds perfect, then."

Emory rushed from her office. "Dirk!"

"Hey, Laurie, I gotta go." He clicked off and reached to touch Emory's arm. "What's wrong."

"I just heard that some children are missing in Carbon County. Two boys and a girl. They were last seen walking home from school."

"Maybe they went to a friend's house and didn't call their parents." Dirk's stomach cramped against the unlikely hope in his words.

"They've called all the friends."

"Do you think it could be Crandall? Or one of the sleezebags who work for him?"

"God, I hope not."

"I'll call Sheriff Donnelly—see what he has so far." Dirk grabbed his phone.

On the third ring, the receptionist answered. "Carbon County Sheriff's Department."

"This is Deputy Marshal Sterling from Billings. I need to speak with the sheriff, right away."

"Hold please." Irritating, overly upbeat music blared

into his ear while he waited until the woman returned to the call. "I'm sorry, but Sheriff Donnelly is unavailable right now. Can I take a message?"

"I'm calling about the missing children from Edgar. Is there anything we can do to support your search?"

"Not yet. We won't be asking for community volunteers to assist in searches until the kids have been missing for a few more hours. Our deputies are in the process of checking with all their friends and the shops to see if anyone has seen them. If we end up having to employ a search team, we'd be glad for your help."

"How old are the kids?"

"Elementary school aged."

"You should reach out to the FBI. They handle missing children eleven and younger."

"I'm sure the sheriff will do just that. Thank you."

"Please keep me posted." Dirk gave her his contact information. "We want to help any way we can."

Emory hovered nearby, listening to his side of the conversation. "Those poor parents."

"Yeah." Dirk knew the pain of losing a child—a horror he wouldn't wish on anyone. "While we wait to hear, Hank and I are going to go to the casino."

"What?" Emory's face held confused shock, which made Dirk laugh.

"Not to gamble. Come on." He motioned for Hank to come with him. "I want to talk to the management and ask if they've had any unusually large transactions lately."

"Why?"

"Because one of Crandall's business pillars was money laundering. If he's setting up shop in Montana, he might be cleaning his funds through the casino. It's a common practice."

Hank followed Dirk out to a black SUV owned by the Marshals Service. It was the vehicle Dirk drove for work when he rode his bike to the office. Hank hadn't been to a casino since he went to Las Vegas with his family back when he was in high school. They hadn't allowed him to hang out in the rooms filled with light-blinking, bell-ringing games, but what he had seen of it appeared glamorous. He looked forward to seeing the games again with adult eyes.

"How does someone go about using a casino to launder money?" Hank asked.

"He'd buy a large dollar amount of chips with the tainted cash and then spend a couple of hours gambling over the course of a week or so. At the end of the designated time, after the money they put into the system gets redistributed, the guy will return and cash in his chips for clean money a little bit at a time, so the IRS doesn't get notified."

Dirk pulled into the dirt parking lot of a brown building that resembled a big barn with a glass entryway. A flashing sign outside the building with the word Casino blinked on and off. If the garish neon script hadn't been hanging over the door, he would never have guessed this was the place.

Hank peered out the window. "This isn't what I was expecting."

"You sound disappointed," Dirk said as he parked the Explorer.

"No, just surprised."

"You expected Caesar's Palace, or the MGM Grand?"

Hank shrugged. "Yeah, sorta."

His shoulders drooped further when they went inside. The dimly lit large room held three rows of slot machines and other mechanical games. There was a self-serve soft drink station next to a popcorn machine on one wall and a small bar on another. The back wall hosted a counter where patrons bought their chips for poker, blackjack, craps, and roulette. The only aspects of the place that resembled what he'd expected were the dings and bings of the electronic machines and the suffocating smell of stale cigarette smoke.

Hank stayed with Dirk as he strode past the games and approached a carpeted staircase in the back next to the cashiers. A Native American guard stepped forward to block their access. "The upstairs is off limits."

"Not to us." Dirk flashed his silver-star badge. "Deputy US Marshals Sterling and Flannigan. We're here to see whoever is in charge."

"You got a federal warrant? Cuz if not, you're not going up these stairs." The guard puffed his chest into Dirk's taller frame. Lucky for the man, Dirk chose not to engage.

"I just want to ask your boss a few questions. The type that will help him avoid the necessity of us having to get that warrant."

A stately man dressed in a three-piece suit descended the stairs. His black hair was cut short and neat. He tugged on his coat and shot his cuffs displaying silver and turquoise cufflinks that matched the rings on his fingers. "It's alright, Ben, we don't want to give these friendly cops any reason to question our business here. We have nothing to hide."

"We're not cops. We're Deputy US Marshals, and we're not here to investigate your business. At least not in the way you mean." Dirk shook the man's hand and introduced himself and Hank once again, building rapport with him.

"I'm Alec Nashoba. I'm the CEO of this casino. Please, come up to my office. It's quieter there and we can talk." The stoic Crow man gave his guard a meaningful look. "See to it no one disturbs us."

"Yes, sir."

The three men climbed the stairs to the casino office, which was a large room with a bank of monitor screens on one side and a bare-bones business suite on the other. Two more native men sat on a sofa in front of a picture window.

"Please, have a seat and tell me what this is all about."

Hank sat in a chair in front of Nashoba's desk, but Dirk remained standing.

"Have you heard about the kids who've gone missing over in Edgar?"

The man frowned and shook his head. "No. Can't say that I have. Why? What does that have to do with our casino?"

"Nothing, I hope. But we're trying to track down a man we believe to be involved in human trafficking and money laundering."

"Ah. You think he's pushing tainted cash through our operation?"

"It's possible. Have you noticed anyone buying large amounts of chips lately? More than usual?"

"Nothing that stands out, but I can have my accountant check the books."

"Please do. And have him look for someone cashing in chips for large sums, too."

"I will ask him to go through the accounts right away. We don't want to be party to anything illegal. Of course."

Hank couldn't tell for sure, but he thought he detected something less than authentic in the man's tone. He glanced at Dirk to see if he caught it too.

"Of course not. And since that's the case, I'm sure you wouldn't mind a forensic accountant going over your books with him?"

"I don't think you mentioned having a warrant."

"Do you need me to get one? If you have nothing to hide, it should be a simple search."

"Yes. You will need a warrant to see our books, Deputy Marshal. And now, I must ask you to leave as I have a meeting in a few minutes. I hope you have a nice afternoon." Nashoba offered his hand.

The two men on the couch stood and followed Hank and Dirk to the door. As they descended the stairs, Hank noticed a woman he recognized playing at the roulette wheel. "Hey, Sterling. Isn't that Molly? The woman from the bar in Edgar?"

Dirk's intense gaze scanned the room below until they found the woman Hank pointed to. "Yes. Molly Briggs. She's the woman sleeping with Johnny aka Beaux Crandall. And if I were a gambling man, I'd bet Molly doesn't make enough to be playing roulette like a high roller." Dirk ducked behind the first row of slots, pulling Hank with him. "Walking through here together, we look like a couple of cops. You have a friendly look to you, so you go talk to Molly. I'll stay back here out of sight. Find out what she's doing here in the middle of the day."

Hank stopped to watch an old man playing a traditional slot machine before he approached the spinning wheel, its silver ball bouncing onto the red eight. "Molly?" She glanced at him as she set down a small stack of chips. "That's your name, right? Nice to see you again. It's me, Hank. We met at the bar in Edgar the other afternoon."

Molly gave him a once-over, and her gaze shifted behind him, probably looking for his friend. "Yeah, that's me."

"Having any luck?" He shoved his hands in his pockets and looked at her from underneath a flop of bangs.

"Nah." She relaxed in response to his easy-going manner. "This game is for losers. I never win."

"I've heard roulette is purely a game of luck and that you have a better chance to win with poker or blackjack."

"You a card shark or something?" She grinned, and the lines on her face aged her by ten years.

Hank laughed with her. "Hardly. But I'd like to try it out. Want to play together?"

"I guess. My luck can't get any worse. I usually stick to the roulette wheel and the slots, but today, I'll be adventurous."

Hank pulled out a chair at the blackjack table for her. "You come here a lot?"

"It's the only fun thing to do around here when I'm not working."

"Gamble away your tip money?" Hank winked and gave her his most charming smile.

"No." Molly sat straight up and wiggled her backend onto the seat. "As a matter of fact, my boyfriend likes to spoil me with an occasional bundle of cash. He tells me to spend it all on chips and have some fun. At least he thinks I'm worth it." She pointed to two long trays filled mostly with hundred-dollar chips.

Bingo. Hank's shoulders tingled at the sight of so many pricey chips. Hopefully, Dirk was watching all this. "Sounds like he cares a lot for you. You're lucky."

"Uh oh. You sound like a man with a broken heart."

Hank wished his raw emotions in that realm were fake, but unfortunately, he could talk about his painful relationship with authenticity. Amy had told him she wasn't planning on coming home from her mother's anytime soon.

"I guess you could say that. It's why I'm here on my day off, instead of at home."

Molly rested her fingers on his forearm. "I'm sorry to hear that. It'll all work out. And if it doesn't, it's her loss."

"Thanks for saying so, but I don't agree. I already miss her like crazy."

Molly raised her hand to call a server over. "Can we get some drinks? I'll have a rum and Coke." She turned to Hank. "You?"

"I'll have an IPA if you have one," he told the server. She nodded and jotted on her pad and went to collect their order.

Hank and Molly played two rounds before she said it was time for her to leave for work. "I should probably cash these chips in. I've been wandering around with them weighing down my purse for too long. Thanks for the games. I hope to see you at the bar again soon."

"You can count on it. See ya later."

As soon as Molly left the casino with cash in hand, Dirk joined Hank at the blackjack table. "That was interesting."

"I think we've found our laundrywoman."

CHAPTER 11

irk and Hank left the casino after Molly did and drove over to Edgar for lunch. They stopped at the diner they had visited before.

"Are you going to order smiley-faced pancakes this time?" Hank smirked.

"Ha ha." Dirk kept his expression stoic. "I can't help it if I have happy childhood memories of a diner just like this one. And you know what? I might just order those smile-cakes in spite of your judgment."

Laughing, Hank held up his hands in surrender. "No judgment here."

They entered the restaurant and asked to be seated in the back. Both he and Hank slid into a circle booth and sat near the center facing the door. It was a habit of their trade. Dirk was only comfortable if he could see all the entrances and exits.

No sooner had their waitress set down their lunch plates—one with Hank's burger and fries and the other with a smiling bacon face on a stack of pancakes and whipped cream curls—than Sheriff Donnelly entered the diner. Dirk picked up half the bacon smile and bit into its crispy saltiness.

He pointed with the remainder of the strip still in his fingers. "Look who just walked in."

Hank raised his gaze from his plate. "Small world."

"And an even smaller county."

The sheriff noticed them and ambled over to their table. His brows worked up and down when he looked at Dirk's plate. "Have I interrupted playtime?"

"Not at all. You're welcome to join us, if you want," Dirk invited.

"No thanks. I'm meeting someone. I heard you called my office this morning."

"Yeah." Dirk dropped the bacon and wiped the grease from his fingers. "I wanted to see how you were doing with the case of those missing kids."

Donnelly frowned and wagged his head. "Haven't seen hide nor hair of any of them."

"We'd like to help you search when the time comes. In fact, another marshal friend of mine has a K9 partner we could bring in for tracking."

"Thanks for the offer, but we've got it covered." Donnelly nodded at two men entering the diner. "We don't need the feds taking over a job we can do just fine on our own. Those are the men I'm meeting for lunch, so I better go."

"We're just trying to help, Sheriff. Ultimately, it won't be us who takes over. But I have no doubt you'll hear from the FBI. Missing children under the age of twelve are their domain," Dirk said to the man's back as he walked away.

The lawman stopped and looked over his shoulder.

"The best thing you can do to help is stay out of it, and I'll say the same thing to the FBI if they try to butt in."

Hank's mouth fell open. "What an ass. What do you suppose that's about?"

"Who knows? He's clearly got a hard-on for federal agencies. It's not unheard of. Local guys seem to think the feds want to come in and take over their cases. Which isn't the truth. More often than not, the various agencies simply have more resources. Smart sheriffs understand that and take advantage of it."

Hank lifted his burger with both hands. "Guess he's not one of them," he said before he sank his teeth into an enormous bite.

Dirk's stomach rumbled, envious of the juicy sandwich Hank was clearly enjoying and he called the waitress over. "I've changed my mind. I think I'll have a burger and fries too."

The older woman smiled kindly. "Flap jacks not giving you enough to go on? No problem, honey. I'll take that off your bill and bring you that burger."

"No need. I'm happy to pay for it, but you're right. I need something with a little more drive power."

After lunch, Dirk took the bill up to the counter to pay. The waitress had removed his pancake face off the tab, so he tipped her generously and added the cost of the kid's meal to the gratuity. "Thanks, Bella."

"You're welcome, honey. You all come back real soon, okay?"

"Count on it." Dirk noticed Donnelly watching them as they left. Something was off about that guy, and it wasn't only his anti-feds attitude.

Once they were in the car, Dirk suggested going to

Molly's bar. "We can say you ran into me at the casino, and we thought it would be fun to stop in for a beer and to say hi."

Hank scrolled through his phone. "Sounds good, but what are you hoping to find?"

"Maybe we'll get lucky and her boyfriend, 'Johnny', will show up." Dirk watched Hank swipe his screen. "Any word from Amy?"

"No." He slid the phone into his pocket. "It's like she's flipped a switch."

"What do you mean?"

"For the last six months, she's been all about taking her temperature and having sex at the right time so she can get pregnant. Always mad that I'm not home enough. Then, all of the sudden, she's gone. It's like she gave up and doesn't even want to talk to me. I call her all the time, but I'm just sent to voicemail."

"Have you tried driving over to her mom's house to talk to her?"

"No." Hank slumped in his chair. "I'm afraid she'll tell me we're over."

"I doubt that."

"I'm just going to give her some space. She can call me when she's ready."

Poor kid. Watching him go through his personal misery made Dirk's chest tight. Relationship stress was the worst. "It's almost three, which makes it five o'clock on the East Coast. First round is on me." Dirk parked the SUV in front of the bar, and they went inside.

Molly saw them come in through the door and waved. "Twice in one day. I wish I'd of had that kind of luck at the roulette table this morning." She set two cocktail napkins on the bar. "Another rum and Coke?"

Hank shook his head. "How about a bourbon straight up with a beer chaser?"

"Uh oh. Lose your shirt at the casino?"

"Nah. But it looks like I might end up losing more than my shirt here pretty soon."

Molly's face bunched in concern, and she patted his hand. "I'll make it a double, on the house."

The bar door opened, letting in a blinding slash of sunlight that silhouetted two men wearing cowboy hats and gun belts. The door closed, and it took a couple of seconds for Dirk's eyes to readjust to the dim light and to realize the men were sheriff's deputies.

Dirk added an IPA to Hank's order, and when Molly went to get their drinks, he clapped Hank on the shoulder. "Don't give up so easily, man. You should go to Amy and talk this through. Waiting for her to make the first move is a bad idea."

"What do you know?" Hank sounded like a surly nine-year-old.

Dirk moistened his lower lip and rolled it between his teeth. Whatever he was willing to share with Hank, it wasn't much. "I've made my mistakes, and not making sure my wife knew how much I loved her was one of my biggest ones. Take that for what it's worth."

Molly returned, saving Dirk from having to say more. "Here you go, boys. Do you want anything from the kitchen? Maybe some buffalo wings?"

"No thanks," Hank answered. "After I ran into Dirk, we had lunch at the diner a little while ago. We just thought we'd stop in and say hi before we headed out of town."

"How sweet. If I wasn't already attached, I'd kiss you right on the mouth." Molly giggled like a young girl and poured some snack mix into a bowl. She set it on the bar between them. Hank's cheeks flushed, which set Molly off in more giggles.

Dirk chose a rye toast circle out of the mix and popped it in his mouth. "You're quite the charmer. I'm gonna have to start calling you LK, short for Lady Killer."

At the far end of the bar, Molly answered a call on her phone, and Dirk watched her over the rim of his pint glass. The color on her face deepened and she glanced at herself in the bar-back mirror. She ran her fingers through her bangs and fluffed them.

Dirk tilted his bottle toward the deputies seated at a table near the pool table. "How much you wanna bet that Donnelly sent those boys to keep an eye on us?"

"It'd be a safe bet."

"Let's go have a little chat with them." Dirk took a swig of beer and slid off the stool and Hank followed. They walked straight to the table where the deputies snatched up menus and pretended like they were deciding on their order. "Good evening, Deputies. I don't know if it will help, but you might be able to read the selections better if your menu was right side up."

The deputy caught in the act smirked. "Not real convincing, huh?"

"No, not really." Dirk and his partner took a seat at the deputies' table. "Why are you following us? Is there something you want to ask? It might be easier than following us around hoping to find it out."

"Sorry. I'm Deputy Cody Manning and this is Deputy Dan Olsen. Our sheriff put us on your tail. He wanted us to watch you and find out why you're asking questions all around Edgar and Red Lodge."

After studying Manning, Dirk took another pull from his bottle. "I'm Deputy US Marshal Dirk Sterling and this is my partner, Hank Flannigan. We're hunting a fugitive. We're not sure if he's come through here or not, but, if we find anything, we'll contact the sheriff and bring you guys in on it. Is that that all you needed to know?"

"I guess."

Dirk flipped through the photos on his phone. When he found the one of Crandall, he held it up for the deputies to see. "Have you seen this man in the area?"

Manning took the phone to see the image closer. He shook his head and passed the photo to Olsen. "I've never seen him before."

"Me either," Olsen handed Dirk's phone back.

Dirk pulled a business card from his wallet. "Well, if you do. Will you contact me at the Billings Marshals Office? Here's my cell number." He scrawled the information on the back of the card. "We'd be happy for the help."

"Sure will, and sorry—you know—for the tail."

"You were just doing your job. Have good night fellas." Dirk drained his beer and stood. He and Hank waved to Molly.

"Good night, boys. Don't be strangers!"

CHAPTER 12

Beaux longed for the days when he had a full team in place of men he trusted. Some issues would always require his personal supervision, but lately he was forced to be hands-on at every turn as he built his new business in Montana. It was much harder to find reliable help in the small western towns than it ever had been in the South.

Frustration bubbled under his skin as he waited at the seedy little bar. It was time for him to confront another business problem. He had discovered the perfect gullible pawn in Molly. She attended to his money-laundering without any awareness of how he was using her, and she happily took care of his physical desires as well. But she was stupid and had started running her mouth.

It was ten o'clock at night. The clock dragged its minute hand as he sat sipping a caramel-sweet cognac, waiting for Molly to finish her shift. The woman seemed to know everyone who came into the grungy establishment.

Which wasn't hard to imagine since the population out here in this wild west town was minuscule.

It wasn't the locals she visited with who concerned him, however. It was the two out-of-towners who kept showing up. He suspected they weren't from Edgar, and Molly confirmed his suspicion when she told him the men were from Billings. And that begged the question of why they kept coming to her bar and chatting her up? She spent far too much time with them, and it made him nervous.

When she was ready to leave, Molly wiped the bar a final time, the Pine Sol scent clashing with the buttery undertones of his drink. He tossed back the remaining alcohol in his glass while she untied her apron and went through the swinging door into the kitchen to punch out.

"Ready?" Molly sang as she returned to the stool where he sat. She ran her fingers across his shoulders and leaned down to kiss his cheek.

Beaux brought her hand to his lips and kissed her fingertips. "More than ready."

He stood and led Molly across the saloon to the door and out to his Cadillac. She cooed and simpered over the rich color and the smooth leather interior before she sat in the seat and bounced up and down like a child on a carnival ride. His car was too elegant for the likes of her to ride in, and it mollified him that she knew it.

"Johnny, this car is so gorgeous! You must be super rich."

He closed her door without bothering to respond as irritation swirled to high temperatures in his belly. Molly was blithefully unaware of his dark mood, which suited him fine. She'd be easier to handle if she wasn't afraid. He slid into the driver's seat and pulled out of the pitted parking lot.

"Where are you taking me, tonight?" She held her hands in her lap and bunched her shoulders up to her ears. Did she think the juvenile pose was cute?

Beaux smirked to himself. He supposed it would be cute if she were one of the seven-year-old girls he had lined up. Especially if she was wearing a plaid uniform skirt and pigtails. He'd have to remember his imagined scene when he was directing his next video production. His body stirred with anticipation, but first things first—he had to deal with the disloyal bitch sullying his leather interior.

"So, Molly, tell me more about your new friends."

"New friends?"

"Don't play dumb. I'm talking about those two pretty boys who've been strutting around town. They sure seem to like you. Do I need to be jealous?"

"Oh! You mean Dirk and Hank? No. They're just a couple a good ole boys who tip well, so I flirt a little. That's all. It doesn't mean anything. You have no reason to worry. I promise." Her face paled in the glow of the dashboard, and she picked at a scab on the back of her hand.

"What all have you been talking to them about?"

"We just chat about this and that. Nothing really."

She was avoiding his question and his anger flared. "What exactly do you *chat* about?"

"They've only been in a few times. It's not like we're best friends or anything."

"Answer my question."

Molly stared at her hands—her clutched knuckles

white in her lap. "I swear we don't talk about anything in particular."

"They've never asked you any questions about anyone?"

Molly closed her eyes and swallowed hard. "Well, there was the one time."

"What one time?" Beaux's patience was razor thin.

"The first day I met them, they had a picture. They said they were looking for the man in the photo because he won a prize of some kind."

His blood bubbled hot in his veins, but he kept his voice steady. "And did you tell them who I was?"

"Only your first name." She darted her gaze out the window, and her limbs stiffened.

"What else? What else did you say to them?"

"Nothing." She drew in a breath and held it. Then her words flowed as she released it. "I just said, 'I know him, that's Johnny.'" She slowly turned her head to look at him —her face was drawn and pale. "But that's all I said. I didn't tell them anything else about you. I swear."

Fury flare in Beaux's chest and hot anger shot down his arm. Like a lightning bolt, his arm jerked, and he struck her in the face. "You stupid bitch!"

She was so stunned she didn't cry out, but snot flowed from her nose like a spigot. Her hands flew to her face. "I'm sorry, Johnny. You never told me not to tell anyone that I knew you. I won't talk about you anymore. I didn't know," she cried.

"Damn right, you won't." Beaux pressed on the accelerator, and they surged into the black night. They drove in silence for over an hour, and Molly didn't ask again about where they were going.

He turned onto the gravel road that led to his new Montana log-cabin home. It was just as nice as the one he'd borrowed from his client in Canada, only it wasn't on a lake. However, the mountain view was equally spectacular, especially when the sun set behind the severe jagged peaks on the horizon. But that night, with the mere sliver of moon hiding behind the clouds, he couldn't make out their silhouettes.

The porch lights were on, and Beaux slammed on his brakes, skidding to a stop before the grand front steps. "Get out," he growled at Molly.

She sniffed and opened her door. Beaux marched around his car and grabbed her by the arm. He propelled her up the steps and in through the front door. Troy and Rufus were playing cards and waiting for him inside the main room. They stood when he entered.

"Keep an eye on her." He shoved Molly into a side chair and marched to the bar for a drink. "I want to know everything there is to know about the two men who've been asking around town about me." He slammed back a double shot of bourbon. "Did our shipments arrive today? Have you heard from my new contact?"

Troy hovered over Molly's chair. "He called and said he was on his way here. As far as the merchandise goes, six kids arrived in a moving container this afternoon. They've been washed and put in the room with the others."

"Only six? I thought we ordered eight." Beaux sent a heated glower at his guard.

"Two didn't survive the trip."

"Call the distributor. I am not paying for product I didn't receive." He poured another generous splash of amber liquid into the cut crystal. "And the other? The guns?"

"All firearms are accounted for, sir. There's something reliable about dealing in inanimate objects."

Beaux peered at Troy over the rim of his glass. "Yes. But you can only sell a gun one time. Children? I can sell them over and over and over." The thought both warmed and comforted him.

Molly jumped from the chair. Her eyes popped wide, and her face went crimson. "You're selling *children*?" She barely choked the words out.

"And now that you know, you're going to help me."

"I won't do anything that helps you hurt kids. I can't believe I thought you were a good guy! I am so out of here." She started for the door.

Beaux motioned in her direction with his finger, and Troy snagged her by the waist. He threw her back into the chair. Beaux laughed. "You're not going anywhere. Besides, I plan to make you a film star. A room mother of sorts in my kiddy-porn videos."

Horror filled the brainless woman's face and Beaux laughed.

The front door swung open, and Crandall's newest contact strode in with his thumbs hooked behind his belt buckle. "I got here as fast as I could. What's the fuss?"

"Ted, good to see you. I wonder if you can identify a couple of men that Molly has recently become friendly with."

Ted shifted his gaze from Beaux to Molly, and back. "What men?"

"A dark-haired guy in his early forties and a younger

blond who looks like he's in his twenties. They aren't locals."

"Oh, yeah. I think I know who you're talking about. They've been butting into everybody's business the last couple of days."

Beaux eased his girth onto a bar stool. "Who are they?"

"A couple of Deputy US Marshals out of Billings." Ted approached the bar and held a glass up for a pour. "Why?"

"God damn it!" The bourbon curdled in Beaux's gut. "They've been showing a picture of me around the county and asking a bunch of questions. If they're marshals, then the feds know I'm back in the United States and suspect that I'm somewhere in the area." Beaux lifted the bourbon bottle in question.

Ted set his glass down to receive the booze. "What are you going to do?"

"There's nothing we can do but stay out of sight from now on. And that includes you." Beaux poured two fingers for Ted and sloshed another half a glass of bourbon for himself. There wouldn't be enough hootch in the whole state if the US Marshals had him in their sights. His whole life would be ruined.

The newcomer glanced at Molly. "What about her?"

"Molly? As of tonight, she is a permanent resident in this house." He sneered at her. "I'm going to make her a star. She can take care of my needs *and* keep the brats in line at the same time. I'm surprised I didn't think of it before." Beaux was pleased with how he had turned what could have been a disaster into something that benefited him in every way. He'd always had a knack for bending circumstances in his favor. "But we'll need someone new who can push our cash through the casino."

"There is no way I'm staying here with you, Johnny!" Molly darted for the door.

Rufus took his turn, grabbing a handful of her hair as she ran past him. He yanked her backward off her feet, and she fell, cracking her elbows on the stone tile.

Beaux sauntered over and looked down at her body sprawled out on the floor. "You have no choice, my dear." He ran the point of his cowboy boot down the line of her jaw. He circled the fresh bruise on her cheek and then tapped his toe on her throat. "Don't make me have to teach you to behave. I don't want you bruised and battered before we make our videotapes. A bloodied face *during* the filming, of course, is another thing altogether." He chuckled at the fear seeping into her eyes. "That's right, Molly, my dear. You're wise to be afraid."

"Aren't any of you going to do something to help me?" Molly wailed, appealing to the one man who had yet to hurt her.

Ted smirked. "I expect I'll help by watching the video when you're all done filming."

Pure pleasure gladdened Beaux's bones as he watched the realization of her situation slowly dawn on Molly's stupid face. He deeply enjoyed the moments when his victims began to realize they belonged to him and would live or die according to his mercy.

"There's no one here to help you, Molly." Beaux spoke gently as though to a child. "Troy, take her in to the room with the children. We can deal with all of them tomorrow. Tonight, we need to make a plan to dispose of those nosey deputy marshals."

CHAPTER 13

Dirk waited for Ceylon to emerge from the crowd of people exiting the secured section of Logan International Airport in Billings. He looked forward to seeing the heroic young woman again. His sense of adventure and justice resonated with her brave trip across the Atlantic and up through South America in her quest to stop her father from his mission of terror. Without her efforts, Aydin Rahip would have killed countless thousands more innocent people than he did.

When she arrived, Ceylon stood still among the bustling crowd, searching for him. Dirk raised his hand to get her attention, and a smile lit her olive features when she spotted him. She rushed forward.

"Deputy Sterling!"

"Dirk."

She smiled, and her dark eyes warmed. "Dirk. Thank you for coming to get me."

"Of course. Are you ready for a relaxing time hidden away in the mountains?

"More than you know!"

Dirk took her carry-on bag from her. "Did you check any luggage?"

"No. This is all I have."

"Okay. Let's get you to your retreat home. We've got a little over an hour's drive. Do you need to freshen up or anything before we head out?"

Ceylon lowered her gaze and color saturated her cheeks. Even after all she'd been through, talk of personal matters with a man caused her to blush. Her shyness charmed him. "The women's restroom is across the concourse. I'll wait right here."

Soon they were seated in his Rubicon, driving west toward the Beartooth Mountains. It had been too long since he'd spent time at his cabin getaway, and he was happy to share the remote place with Ceylon. She deserved some time to find her footing after surviving the events of the last months and before she started school at NYU.

"I've planned a dinner party at the cabin tonight to celebrate and welcome you to Montana. Hank will be there, and my boss, Chief Grey, along with a few other friends you haven't met yet."

"I'm honored. Thank you." Ceylon cast her gaze to her lap. "I'm happy to help your wife cook the food. I always helped my mother."

"I'm not married. So, you'll have to deal with *my* grilling skills."

"Oh." Her smile brightened. "I'm sure you will prepare a delicious meal."

"It should be fun." Fun didn't exactly describe how *he* felt about it. The event was more of a point of passage. It was his way of gathering the people he cared about together at one time and forcing himself to move forward. Teresa was the one woman in his life that came with no complications. She and her son would be the easiest guests to host.

Dirk hoped the dinner would give him an opportunity to clear his mind regarding Emory and Laurie. He figured doing it surrounded by friends was the best way to force himself to accept reality. He was meant to be a man living on his own.

Emory didn't want a future with him, so he had to move past that idea. Inviting Dave to come with Emory would compel Dirk and everyone else to recognize those two as a couple. Then there was Laurie, who imagined she wanted to be with him, but Dirk knew she was simply lonely and vulnerable. He was her safety net, but she needed to understand that though he would always be there for her and Caleb, it would only ever be as a friend. There was a line between Laurie and him that Dirk would never cross, even if at times he was tempted. That line was the specter of her deceased husband—his previous partner—Sam. Some things were simply too sacred.

Dirk also hoped that getting Hank and Amy out together for a fun night might help them relax. They'd been under too much strain.

Ceylon stared out the windows with an awed expression and interrupted his thoughts. "These mountains are breathtaking! I've never seen such..." She searched for the word. "Majesty."

"They are, indeed."

"Thank you for sharing this with me."

"I'm happy to. It'll be a great place for you to rest and regroup before you start college."

They stopped in a small mountain town for the groceries he needed for his dinner party. The market was next to the bar where he had first met Emory—the night she told him her name was Shirley. The memory brought a grin to his face, but instead of feeling mirth, his chest filled with a deep ache.

Before long, they turned onto his dirt road and climbed the hill to his private nirvana. Dirk's cabin was moderate-sized, with a master bedroom, an office, a great room on the main floor, and two bedrooms in the loft. "Here we are. Your home for as long as you want to stay."

Ceylon's mouth parted as she stared at the beauty of the place and Dirk saw it all again, fresh through her eyes.

"This place is incredible. Thank you for inviting me to stay here." Ceylon opened the car door and reached for her suitcase.

Dirk was quick to take it from her, and he followed her to the front entrance. "Let me get the door for you." He pulled it open and gestured for her to enter before him. "Your room is at the top of the stairs.

Ceylon spun in a slow circle taking in the vaulted ceiling. Dirk gave her a tour and allowed her some time to get settled while he put away the groceries, keeping out the food he needed for their dinner.

When she joined him in the kitchen, Dirk had bacon frying and was slicing apples for the crisp he was making for dessert. "Let me know if you need anything."

"Dirk, your home is beautiful. It is so generous of you to allow me to stay here."

"Not at all. And remember, I'll only be an hour away."

"When do your dinner guests arrive?"

"Between six and six-thirty. Why don't you rest until then?"

While Ceylon unpacked, Dirk finished prepping the dinner ingredients. Checking the clock, he wiped his hands on the dishtowel and headed for the shower. His guests were due in half an hour.

Hank and Amy were the first to arrive. The mood between them was tense and Amy obviously struggled to meet Dirk's eyes when Hank introduced them.

"It's nice to finally meet you, Amy. Hank talks about you incessantly," Dirk teased, hoping to lighten the atmosphere.

Amy's eyes, which matched her light brown hair, snapped up to his and then darted to Hank. "He does?"

"Yes. You're clearly all he thinks about." Dirk shook Hank's hand and stepped aside to let them in. "Make yourselves at home. Beer's in the fridge and there's wine on the bar."

"Thanks for having us. Great place."

Dirk bobbed his head and ushered them into the great room. He introduced Amy to Ceylon, and then he and Hank went to the kitchen to get drinks started. "How's it going with you two?"

Hank shoved a hand into his hair. "Not great, but at least she agreed to come tonight. That's a start."

"Good. Hopefully, she'll have a nice time and begin to see our team as friends."

The doorbell rang, and Dirk went to answer. Emory stood before him in jeans, hiking boots, and a pink and gray flannel shirt. Her hair fell in loose waves over her shoulders. He stared, and his mouth curled into an appreciative smile. He'd never seen her in casual clothes before.

"Emory. You look fantastic."

Her brows dipped, and she gestured behind her. "Dave told me dinner in the mountains would be casual."

Oh, yeah, *Dave*. "Well, he was right. Hey, Aldrich. Welcome. Go on in and get something to drink. Hank and Amy are talking with Ceylon in the great room, and I see Teresa just pulled in." He let them pass before he went outside to greet his other co-worker and her son.

"Hey, Mendez." He accepted a covered dish from her, and she opened the back door of her car. "Hi, Tomas. How's it going, buddy?"

A cute little black-haired six-year-old leapt from the car and hugged Dirk's waist. "Hi, Dirk!" Then he was off, excitedly exploring the front porch.

"That's a long trip for an active kid. He needs to run off some of his energy before he goes inside." Teresa smiled as her son jumped from the top step to the ground and ran toward them.

"There's nothing in there he can hurt." Dirk led the way into the cabin. He set the casserole dish on the counter and made sure everyone had something to drink. The timer went off on the brie he was baking for the appetizer, and he covered it with a cranberry-onion chutney. He placed the melted cheese platter on the table with a basket of crackers and poured himself two fingers of his favorite single-malt scotch.

Dirk ran through his mental list for the evening. "Hey, Tomas. Want to help me start a fire in the pit out back?"

"Yeah!"

"Good. Let's wait a few minutes until everyone is here,

first." Dirk scanned the small crowd, and his gaze rested on Emory, appreciating the snug fit of her jeans that accentuated her perfect ass. Obviously noticing Dirk's perusal of his date's fine features, Aldrich stepped next to her and slid his arm around her waist. He pulled her close, staking his claim, and Dirk gave himself an internal shake. Telling himself, *Move on, dude.*

The night sky darkened, and he wondered where Laurie and Caleb were. He was about to call her when the doorbell rang. With relief, he went down the hall to answer it. He opened the heavy wooden door and Laurie stood before him in a long black raincoat belted at the waist. She wore extremely high heels, and her hair and make-up looked more appropriate for a fancy dinner, or the theatre in the city.

"Hi. I'm glad you're here. I was getting concerned. You look beautiful. Where's—"

Before he could ask where Caleb was, Laurie bit her red-stained lips nervously. She tugged on the belt and opened her coat. Underneath, she wore only a black-lace bustier and lace panties with garters holding up black silk thigh-highs. Stunned beyond words, Dirk stared at her. Against his will, his body reacted to the vision standing before him.

CHAPTER 14

Emory had been uncomfortable bringing Dave to Dirk's inner sanctum. Especially after their arrival when Dirk didn't even notice Dave standing behind her when he greeted her at the door. It wasn't that Dave was invisible; it was that Dirk's total focus was on her. It was a heady feeling—one she wished she could claim. Dave felt it too and reacted with possessiveness, standing too close, always touching her, drawing her close, and kissing her if he noticed Dirk watching. It was suffocating.

An obvious tension hovered between Hank and his wife, so *he* wasn't an option for escape. Teresa was busy keeping her son out of mischief, and Dirk… well, he was the problem, not the solution. Her best bet was engaging Ceylon in conversation.

"What all have you experienced of America since you got out of the hospital, Ceylon?"

The young woman's fingers moved to her side where she'd been shot, and a sadness filled her eyes, though she forced a brightness into her tone. Of course, she was still grieving her father, even though he had enacted terror on innocent lives. Emory wondered if the young woman would ever fully heal from the mental and emotional trauma.

"I have a governmental agent assigned to me for assistance, and she helped me move into a dorm room at NYU. Most students are gone for the summer, but it made sense for me to move only one time. Although, in truth, I have no real possessions to speak of." Her laugh was soft. "The agent attached to me took me shopping for a few necessities. There are shops on every single street in New York City, I think. It is so much to take in. So many people."

"Yes, but out here in the West, you'll find that life moves a lot slower. This is a nice place for you to relax and find yourself before you go back to the city. I hope you'll call me if you need anything while you're here."

"Thank you. Dirk has already been far too generous. I can hardly believe I get to stay here in his beautiful home." She made a sweeping gesture indicating the whole cabin.

"It is a beautiful place." Emory pictured Dirk living here on weekends and holidays and smiled to herself. He wasn't one to let people into his private life. This dinner was a big step for him.

The doorbell rang, and Dirk left the kitchen to answer it. The only people left to arrive were Laurie Dillinger and her son, Caleb. Emory followed Dirk to the door, using greeting them as another excuse to get a breather from Dave.

———

"Dirk, is that Laurie?" Emory's voice came from behind him, and he responded instantly.

Reaching for Laurie's coat, he closed it around her and tied the belt. "Yeah. It is. She came after an event, so she needs to change. I'll be right back after I take her to my room so she can put on something more casual."

He glanced at Emory and realized he'd been too late. Her face paled and she blinked under raised brows with her mouth opened slightly. She'd seen what Laurie was wearing, and Dirk was at a loss to decipher the swirl of emotions swimming in her eyes. Laurie's face, on the other hand, had gone bright red, and her neck and chest were blotchy with humiliation.

Dirk rushed Laurie into the main-floor master and closed the door behind him. "Laurie..." He had no idea what to say to her.

Tears gathered in her eyes. "Why is *she* here?"

His heart ached for Laurie's embarrassment, but she had completely flabbergasted him. "Emory is part of the team. My whole team is here. Them and Ceylon. Why..." How did he approach her choice in attire?

Laurie pulled the belt of the raincoat tighter and sat on the edge of the bed. She bent over and covered her face in her hands. "Oh, my God! I could just die," she cried into her palms.

"Laurie," Dirk knelt on the carpet before her, "what's all this about?"

She blinked at him, tears spiking her eyelashes. "When you invited me to dinner here, at your cabin... I thought... well, I thought..." She buried her face behind her fingers again.

"But it's a dinner party." The situation had him off kilter.

"You never said anyone else was coming." She muffled her words into her palms.

Dirk's blood ran cold. "I'm pretty sure I did. The dinner is to welcome Ceylon Rahip to Montana."

Her head snapped up, and angry eyes bore into his. "You never told me that. Your text said, and I quote," she fumbled in her purse for her phone and tapped at it furiously. "Hey L, wanna come to my cabin for dinner on Saturday? It'll be late. Might be a good idea to stay over."

"But when we talked, I told you to bring Caleb." His mind raced over the conversation, trying to see where it had gone so wrong.

"And I told you I was taking him to my mom's because..." Accusing eyes flew to his, and her voice dropped to a whisper. "What was I supposed to think? I thought... oh my God! I want to die. And your boss saw me too!" She dissolved into mortified sobs.

Unsure of how to fix this mess, Dirk put his arms around her while she cried. "I'm sorry I wasn't clear, Laurie. I'd been texting all day. I—don't have an excuse. This is my fault." He was such an idiot. "Listen, I'll get you something to wear, and we'll just go with the story about you being at another event before this. Okay?"

"And what about your boss? I'm so embarrassed."

"No. Don't be. I—" Someone rapped softly on his bedroom door. "Hold on."

Dirk went to the door and opened it a crack. Emory stood on the other side. "Can I come in?"

"No. I don't think that's a good idea right now."

—————

Emory wished she had been anywhere but standing there witnessing the woman's humiliation. Dirk was clearly stunned—his smart-assed comments absent from his tongue. The horrified look on Laurie's face told Emory there had been a terrible misunderstanding. She felt the woman's utter mortification in the depth of her bones.

Laurie's eyes had darted to Emory, and she'd yanked her coat closed, belting it tightly. Dirk stepped forward to block anyone from seeing her and with his arm around Laurie's shoulder, he had escorted her quickly into his bedroom.

Emory had no idea why Laurie thought this party was the time to show up and present herself to Dirk on a platter, but she figured there had been a miscommunication on an epic level.

Emory's stomach tightened and her throat thickened with a green, sticky sensation, but she firmly reminded herself Dirk and Laurie's relationship was none of her business. Still, she couldn't help wondering if Dirk would have swept Laurie up in his arms if none of them were there. Did the poor woman get the date of their sleepover mixed up with the date of the dinner party? Were she and Dirk intimately involved? *None of my business!*

Emory noticed Laurie had no overnight bag with her and dashed out to Dave's car to grab her own. She rushed back inside to Dirk's bedroom door. No one else seemed aware of what was happening. Thank God.

She knocked gently on the bedroom door, and seconds later, Dirk opened it a crack. He tried to turn her away, so she pushed her way inside the room. The poor widow had wilted onto the edge of the bed in humiliation.

Doing her best to sound matter of fact, Emory hoped to take the sting out of the situation for Laurie. "Hi, Laurie. I didn't see you carry a bag in, and I figured you must have forgotten yours. I have some clothes in here you can borrow. We're close to the same size, I think."

Emory set her bag on the bed and pulled out a pair of dark brown slacks and a cream jersey tunic. "These should do. Want me to go pour you a glass of wine while you change?"

"I'm so sorry." Laurie's voice wavered as black rivulets of mascara raced down her cheeks.

"I can't imagine what for. I've forgotten my bag before, too. It happens to everyone. I'll just go get you that drink." Emory gave Laurie a kind smile and turned toward the door. She glared at Dirk as she walked by him. "Coming?"

He belatedly realized it was inappropriate for him to remain in the room. "Yeah. I'll uh… Laurie, I'll just be in the other room. Come out when you're ready."

"Emory." Dirk caught her arm and closed the door behind them. He turned her to face him in the bedroom's recessed doorway. She stumbled into him and, holding her breath, looked up into his face. Her heart hammered against her lungs making it hard to breathe.

He stared into her eyes for long seconds before he swallowed. They were too close. His breath brushed across her forehead, and her pulse pounded. His gaze dipped to her mouth, and unable to stand the magnetic pull, Emory closed her eyes and tilted her chin up.

"I'm sorry." He took a step back. "I… I just wanted to thank you for how you handled this thing with Laurie. I don't think I have any clothes that wouldn't fall right off her. Your things will help her pull this off with no one the wiser. You saved her from major embarrassment in front of everyone. That's really kind of you." His eyes held such warmth, she had to look away.

"What made her think…" Emory drew in a deep breath to settle her pulse. She never finished her question. It wasn't any of her business.

"It was my fault. I'd been texting about the party all morning and inadvertently didn't mention that it was a party with a bunch of people. Only that I was cooking dinner here and maybe she should think about staying the night. I only meant that it would be late, and she shouldn't drive. I assumed she'd bring Caleb, and that she knew it was a party." He ran his hand down over his anguished expression. His eyes sought hers for understanding. "Obviously, she thought…"

"Men." Emory shook her head but couldn't keep the smile from her lips—one of genuine relief and of humor. "No one noticed anything, and this will eventually be a funny memory between the two of you. But, honestly, Dirk. I feel so badly for her. She's mortified."

Dirk's humor returned, and his eyes glinted with mischief. "She shouldn't be. She looked damn fine in that getup."

Emory slapped his arm. "Go pour the woman a drink, you jerk." She tried to laugh, but he was still too close. His body heat seeped through her shirt. Her heart pounded with anticipation leaving her breathless and slightly dizzy. She stared into Dirk's deep, dark-gray eyes searching for an answer. Was he feeling this same captivating pull?

Confirmation came as his gaze dipped to her mouth again, and touching her chin, he bent toward her.

Dave appeared in the hallway. "I wondered where you wandered off to." His expression was accusing as his gaze shifted between her and Dirk. His possessiveness was getting tiresome, and they'd only been here an hour. The overnight thing was quickly losing its appeal. Especially with Dirk so nearby.

"I just wanted to say hello to Laurie Dillinger. She's changing, but she'll be right out." Emory walked away, leaving both men behind her, not caring what they had to say to each other, if anything. When she entered the great room, Ceylon was pouring water into glasses on the dinner table.

Eventually, Laurie came out of the bedroom and all the guests congregated in the kitchen area mingling together as though everything was completely normal.

The food Dirk prepared was astonishingly excellent. The steak was juicy and cooked to perfection. Over dinner and drinks, the guests relaxed into easy conversations. The concerned creases on Ceylon's face seemed to smooth as she engaged with everyone.

Laurie took a seat at the dinner table next to Emory and under the table, gripped her hand. "Thank you," she whispered.

Emory squeezed her hand in return and smiled. "We girls have to stick together."

Before long, Amy seemed to relax and enjoy herself. She stopped moving away from Hank's touch. The evasive maneuvers moved from Amy to Emory who suddenly wanted nothing more than to avoid Dave's ever-present hands. He was suffocating her with his attention.

Tomas sat between his mother and Dirk, whose presence seemed to encourage the boy to mind his manners. It took no more than an arched black brow to stop Tomas in the middle of mischief. Dirk's easy rapport with the little boy surprised Emory. She'd never taken him for someone who liked kids. What a strange evening it had turned out to be.

After dinner, Dirk served warm apple crisp topped with vanilla ice cream, and Emory groaned with pleasure as she savored the confection. "You made this yourself, Dirk?"

His slate-colored eyes turned to her. "You sound surprised."

"I guess I am, a little." She took another bite.

"It was my grandma's recipe." Dirk poured more wine into everyone's glass and took his seat at the head of the table. He leaned close to Emory. "Hey, not to bring up work at a party, Chief, but I want to catch you up on what Hank and I think we stumbled onto in Edgar. We met a woman who's dating the man in our photo. The one of Beaux Crandall. Her name is Molly Briggs. She's a bartender at the local watering hole and seems completely unaware that she's hooked up with a drug-pushing, gun-smuggling, pervert. We believe he's using her to launder money through the Reservation Casino."

"Among other things," Hank added wryly as he scooted into the conversation.

Dirk bobbed his head in agreement. "We've become friendly with her, so hopefully we can squeeze more information from her without her suspecting anything."

"Your instincts were right, then," Emory admitted. "Crandall *is* setting up business here in Montana. I'm impressed, Sterling." Their eyes met, and a strong jolt sparked between them. She dropped her gaze to her wineglass, escaping the electric current. When she looked up again, it was at Hank. "Good work, guys. What's your next step?"

Hank deferred to Dirk, who answered, "We'll follow her after she gets off work. See if she'll lead us to Crandall."

"Sounds simple."

Hank smirked. "That's what happens with guys like Crandall. They get cocky—think they're untouchable—and bam! We nab them."

Emory smiled at his exuberance. He was right. When fugitives thought they were smarter than everyone else, they made stupid mistakes.

Ceylon, who had spent the day traveling yawned, and too soon, the dinner party came to an end. Most folks wanted to leave early enough to drive the hour-plus back to Billings. Teresa and Tomas left first, followed closely by Hank and Amy. Emory hoped Hank's wife had a nice time and felt less threatened by them. She wanted Amy to feel like part of their little work family.

Growing up in the Marine Corps, Emory had a deep appreciation for the bonds between the service members' families. They gave each other strength and support to get through the tough times, and she wanted to build her team after that model.

"Ready to go, sweetheart?" Dave slid his arm around her, resting his hand on her hip. She stepped away. "Yes, I just need to get my purse and bag." She strode to Dirk's bedroom to retrieve her things.

Dirk followed her. "Hey, Emory, thanks again. You

rescued the evening for Laurie and allowed her to save face. That means a lot."

"No problem." He was right behind her as she bent to get her bag. His heat sent chills across the surface of her skin. "Laurie is part of the marshal family and a sweet girl."

When she stood, Dirk's hands cupped her shoulders, and he turned her to face him. "Not a lot of women would have been as kind as you were, given the situation. So, seriously. Thank you." He drew her into an embrace, and she lost her breath.

"Hope I'm not interrupting anything." Dave's voice dissipated the magic, and Emory stepped away.

"Not at all. We were just saying goodbye." Emory raised her chin and strode from the room with as much composure as she could muster on shaky knees.

Laurie met her in the hallway to the front door. "I'm staying over tonight. I've had too much wine to drive down the canyon. If you don't mind, I'll have your things cleaned and bring them by the office next week?"

"That's fine." Emory briefly wondered if Laurie's lingerie would reappear later that night. *Still—none of my business.* Though Emory knew the lacy bits she had packed in her bag for the weekend would not make their way into play. Not that night, at least.

Dirk and Dave joined Emory at the door to say good-night. The men shook hands and Dirk kissed her cheek. She breathed in his subtle outdoorsy aftershave. "Thanks again for a lovely time. See you Monday."

Dave drove them down the gravel road toward the highway. "I made reservations at the Beartooth Mountain Inn. It's about twenty minutes away."

"Would you mind if we just went home, instead? I'm sorry, but I'm just too tired."

"Too tired? Or too distracted?"

"What do you mean?" she asked.

"I think you know what I mean. Everyone in the room could see the attraction between you and Sterling."

"You're imagining things." He wasn't, but she denied it anyway. Yes, there was an attraction, but they had decided not to pursue it. Not really. The implications were too dangerous. Neither one of them wanted to put their career in jeopardy, which could happen if desire took a wrong turn in the workplace.

"You know I'm not. At least have enough respect for me to be honest, Emory."

She closed her eyes. "There will never be anything besides professionalism between Dirk and me. That is honest."

"Okay. So, how about we still take that room at the inn, then? No pressure. We can rest tonight and see how we feel about things in the morning. We have all day off tomorrow. I thought maybe we could have a picnic. Maybe some space from… everyone will give us a better perspective on *our* relationship."

"Actually, that sounds nice, Dave. Thanks for understanding." He was a really good guy. She needed to focus on that.

CHAPTER 15

On their drive home, Amy slid her hand onto Hank's leg. He glanced at her from the corner of his eye, and she smiled. His pulse leapt. It was the first time she had initiated touching him since she'd left for her mother's house.

He covered her fingers with his palm. "Did you have a nice time, tonight?"

"I did. And it helps to know your team a little better. Even Dirk, though I'm not sure I'll ever have the power over you that he does."

"He doesn't have power over me, sweetheart. He has my respect."

Amy nodded and slid her hand higher on his leg. He responded by pressing on the accelerator.

"I want to tell you again how sorry I am for everything that happened between us. I'm sorry I hurt you. I want you to be happy. I was being selfish."

"I forgive you. I'm just glad we're on the same page now."

Hank swallowed his uncertainty which was easy to do when all his attention was focused on the location of his wife's hand. "Me too."

As soon as they opened the door to their apartment, Hank pulled Amy into his arms and kissed her with all the longing their time apart had built in him. He lifted her and pushed her against the wall. His emotions welled up into a fiery passion he was desperate to quench. They say, 'makeup sex is the best', and he was determined to prove the statement.

They bumped into the entry table causing the small lamp lighting the hallway to crash on the floor. Amy laughed and whispered, "Take me to the bedroom."

Her wish was his command, but he only made it to the living room couch. It wasn't until hours later that, holding hands, they found their way to their bed.

———

Dave was good to his word and though they shared a bed, he did not make any overt moves. Emory was up early, showered and dressed before Dave woke. Disappointment darkened his eyes before he shuttered the emotion.

"You're a morning person, aren't you?" He smirked.

Emory zipped her bootie. "Guilty. Always have been. Sorry, no matter how late I get to bed, I can't sleep past five. The hazard of being the daughter of a Marine." She kept her tone bright, pretending not to notice his mood. Giving him privacy, she turned her back when he threw back the sheets and plodded to the bathroom.

While he was in the shower, her phone buzzed. "Good morning, ma'am. This is Deputy Cody Manning from the

Carbon County Sheriff's Department. I hate to bother you on a Sunday, but we have overwhelming evidence that leads us to believe a substantial drug deal is going down at a ranch between Roberts and Red Lodge tonight. We're ready to respond, but, if possible, we'd love to have your back-up. The sheriff is out of town and there's only the two of us deputies here."

"What evidence do you have? Tell me why you think the deal is happening tonight?"

"One of our drunk tank regulars has been running at the mouth. Funny the things you can learn when you pull a guy out of the gutter. He's a small-time user—doesn't have the budget for more—but he sounded impressed by the load his dealer was going to bring in. He mentioned the Flying W Ranch, so we think the transaction will happen there. That part is only speculation, but I'd hate to get out there tonight and find we were out gunned."

"I understand, but chatter from a drunk guy is unreliable, at best."

"Yes, ma'am. But if the deal happens and we aren't there, all those drugs filter out into our community. It seems worth the chance. I guess, I understand if you don't want to send back-up all the way out here on a maybe."

"All drug deals are maybes, deputy. I get it. You'll need to fill out a USM-560 Case Delegation Form requesting our assistance. Email the form to me right away so I can approve it. After that, I can send two men from my team down there later today. You can walk them through your plan from there."

"Yes, ma'am. I'll get that to you right away."

"Have you contacted the DEA?"

"I don't think the deal's big enough to bring in

multiple agencies. We just need some back-up, so thanks for your help."

Emory started to dial Dirk, but Dave came out of the bathroom with a towel wrapped low on his hips. He was fit and had clean-cut good looks. Any woman would find him attractive. She focused on his attributes and did her best not to compare him to Dirk. Dave crossed the room and took her hand. Drawing her to her feet, he took her face in his hands and kissed her, pulling her against his damp chest. She tried to relax into him, but her body stiffened.

"What's wrong?" he asked into her hair.

Think it, do it, be it. "Nothing." Emory ran her hands up his back and held him. "Just a work call. Fugitives never sleep."

"But they can wait." He kissed her again. "You can't work twenty-four hours a day." He slid a hand under her shirt and his towel fell.

"Dave, come on." She stepped away. "I thought we were going to go on a picnic—take some time to gain perspective."

"I *have* perspective." His voice dropped as he reached for the towel. "Do you?" Without covering himself, he walked back to the bathroom to get dressed.

Could she screw things up any worse? What was she doing? She raised her voice so he could hear her. "I just have to call my team and give them their assignment. Then we can go to the market for picnic food." He didn't respond. "If you still want to?"

He came out of the bathroom dressed in jeans and a T-shirt. "Say hi to Dirk for me."

"Dave, it's a work call."

"Yeah. I get it."

Guilt flooded through her. She liked Dave a lot and was wrecking things between them because of some stupid crush she felt for a man she could not pursue. "Hey —I'm sorry. I've been distracted, but as soon as I task the guys with their job today, maybe we can start again?"

"Start what?" His stung pride made him surly.

Moving forward with determination, she approached him and splayed her hand across his muscled chest. "For starters, I don't think you were wearing this." She plucked at the fabric of his shirt.

Heat ignited in his eyes as he gathered her into his arms.

CHAPTER 16

Dirk stood barefoot in his kitchen in front of the stove wearing worn jeans and an unbuttoned flannel shirt. Eggs popped in bacon grease as he slid four pieces of bread into the toaster. He hadn't slept well. Guilt over the mess he'd made with the women in his life kept him tossing and turning. Somehow, he had led Laurie to believe that when she arrived last night, it was for an intimate evening together. The last thing he wanted was to hurt or embarrass her, yet the previous night he did both things—times ten.

With all the guests in his cabin, he hadn't paid enough attention to Ceylon. But at least he could remedy that today. He hoped that she'd feel at home and enjoy the breath-taking scenery of the mountains before she flew back to New York. It seemed like she had fun at the dinner, but she had tired early and went to bed.

The most unnerving of all was Emory. Her quick action and her grace with Laurie the night before bowled him over. She effortlessly saved the evening for them all. And as a result, he'd almost kissed her—twice. Damn. And she was at the party with another man, too.

His behavior pissed him off. He was not that kind of a guy. Well, at least he didn't want to be. Though, if he was honest with himself—if Emory would have given him any encouragement at all—he'd have swept her into his room and locked the door, dinner and company be damned. He felt out of control around her and hated not having an iron grasp on himself. The feelings he had swirling inside were dangerous, and he had to do something to shake them.

He flipped the eggs with more energy than necessary, and specks of grease flew from the pan, burning tiny spots on his hand, forearm, and chest. He growled and rubbed the pain away.

"Careful." Laurie slid onto a barstool at the counter behind him. "Don't blame the eggs, the grease will bite back."

"Hey. Good morning. Did you sleep okay?" He removed the skillet from the stove and slid the eggs onto a plate. Setting it in front of Laurie, he noticed she'd washed the makeup from her face. She looked younger—innocent and sweet. He poured her some orange juice. "Bacon?"

"Thanks." She yawned. "I didn't sleep much, to be honest. Listen, Dirk, I'm really sorry about last night."

He did not want to talk about it. "No worries. In the end, I think everyone had a good time, don't you?"

"Look at me."

He let out a puff of air and turned. "Really, Laurie. The whole thing was my fault. I'm the one who's sorry. I love you and Caleb. I'd do anything for either of you, but—"

"But you don't want me." Her voice was small and filled with sorrow. It stabbed Dirk's heart.

"It's not that. It's..." How could he explain? He wasn't sure what his feelings for Laurie were. If no one else was at his cabin when she showed up, would he have turned her away? Not likely. *Shit!* He raked his hair back with his hand and leaned against the counter's edge.

"It's that you have feelings for Emory. Is that it?"

"No!" He jammed his hands into his jean's pockets. "The truth is, I don't want to be in a committed relationship with anyone. And you deserve nothing less than a man who will give you everything. I will always be there for you and Caleb, but I can't offer you the type of commitment you're looking for."

Laurie rolled her lips between her teeth and bit down as if preventing her thoughts from turning into words. Finally, she spoke. "I understand. I hope that changes one day. I—we—Caleb and I, love you too. Obviously, I'd like it to be more than what we have."

Her eyes were clear and her gaze direct. Dirk admired her. She was brave to stay last night and even braver to face him so honestly that morning. "That part of my heart is dead, Laurie. After what I went through after our baby died, and Hannah..." His eyes pricked and he turned his back to her.

"And Hannah broke your heart..."

"Tore my heart out, more like." He faced Laurie again. "I can't go there. Ever again."

Laurie stood and padded into the kitchen. She slid her arms around his waist and pressed her cheek against his back for a moment before turning him and stretching up on her toes to kiss his dark morning-stubbled jaw. "I'm sorry Hannah hurt you so badly, Dirk. But you're giving her far too much power in your life if you let her ruin the rest of it."

The truth of her words slapped him, but he'd be a fool if he ever put himself in a situation where a woman could destroy him again. Not happening. Besides, he was happy as he was. His life wasn't ruined. *Was it?*

The doorbell rang, startling him out of his thoughts. No one ever 'dropped by' way up there in the mountains. He planted a friendly kiss on the top of Laurie's head and moved past her down the hallway—spatula in hand. He swung open the door.

Emory. His pulse hesitated and then catapulted ahead several paces before he found his voice. "Are you okay?" He couldn't imagine what she was doing on his doorstep. "Where's Dave?" If Aldrich hurt her, Dirk would kill him.

"I'm fine," she said, but she didn't meet his gaze. Instead, she pushed her way past him. That's when he saw Dave leaning against his car with his arms crossed over his chest, wearing a cocky grin.

"Morning, Sterling."

"What's going on?" Dirk stepped out onto the porch.

"Em tried to call you, but apparently you never answered your phone."

Em? She lets him call her Em, now? The man's smile grew as he swaggered a few steps toward Dirk. Something about the guy made Dirk want to punch him simply for good measure. Instead, Dirk elected to turn his back on the man and find Emory. He entered the cabin, and with a degree of satisfaction, closed the door leaving Aldrich outside.

Dirk found Emory sitting next to Laurie on one of the

stools in the kitchen. She had poured herself a cup of coffee. Lifting it, she said, "Hope you don't mind."

"Help yourself. Want breakfast?"

"No thanks." She looked at her mug and then around the great room. Anywhere but at him. "Sorry to intrude. I tried to call, but you never answered."

"Sorry. Are you okay?"

"It's not about me. I got a call from a Carbon County sheriff's deputy. They need back-up on a drug deal they believe is going to happen tonight. I told him you and Henry would be there to help."

"The deputy? Not the sheriff?" That was odd.

"I guess the sheriff is out of town. They're worried about being outgunned."

"Sure. Not a problem. I'll get a hold of Hank." Dirk stepped forward and touched Emory's arm. "What else is going on?"

She took a long sip of coffee before she set the cup on the counter and slid off the barstool, away from him. "Nothing. That's it. Call me after it's over. Let me know what happened." She pushed past him and made a beeline to the front door.

"Emory," he hollered after her.

She called over her shoulder, "I'll talk to you later, Dirk. Thanks again for last night." And she was gone, slipping out the door before he could respond.

Laurie gave him a nudge. "Go after her."

He blinked at her words and shook his head. "No need. She's got Aldrich outside waiting for her." He tossed the spatula in the sink so hard it flew out the other side and clattered to the floor. He cleared his throat. "More coffee?"

Ceylon plodded down the stairs in fuzzy slippers and pink pjs. "Good morning. Did I hear Chief Grey's voice?"

"You did. She just stopped by to assign me to a job. We'll be out of your hair in about an hour and then you'll have the place to yourself. How does that sound?"

Ceylon took the seat Emory vacated. "A little lonely. It will be nice for a while, but maybe I can come to Billings and see everyone again, soon."

Laurie poured a cup of coffee for Ceylon. "You are welcome to hang out with me, if you don't mind spending time with a high-energy boy and his dog."

"I'd love it! Thank you."

After dishing up breakfast for Ceylon, Dirk left the women to make their plans while he stewed about Emory and Aldrich. Something had changed. Why wouldn't she look at him? He filled the sink to wash dishes when a cold splash of reality hit him square in the jaw. He dropped the mug he'd been drying, and it broke into pieces on the floor around his bare feet.

CHAPTER 17

That morning, Hank and Amy slept in. He woke first and left the bed to make coffee and cook pancakes for breakfast. He carried a tray with the food into the bedroom and woke Amy with the enticing aroma of the dark roast.

"I can't drink coffee, Hank." Her tone was cooler than he'd expected.

"Don't worry. Yours is decaf."

"Oh. Well, that's good, then." She sipped from the cup he handed her.

Setting the tray on the bed, he bent to kiss her. "Last night was amazing. I missed you so much. Let's never fight again."

"I agree." Amy dug into her pancakes with gusto making Hank laugh.

"You must have worked up a big appetite."

"I did, and it's nice to have breakfast served to me in bed." She took another bite.

After they finished, Hank stacked their plates on the

tray and set it on the floor. He crawled back under the sheets, pulling Amy on top of him. He rolled her over, exchanging positions and he kissed her with growing heat, tasting her maple syrup sweet lips.

His phone rang, but the ringtone sounded distant. He ignored it and continued kissing his wife until it stopped. It rang again.

Amy pushed against his chest and slid out from under him. She rummaged in the pile of their clothes from the night before and found his device. The skin on her face tightened and her eyebrows rose with accusation as she held the screen up to him.

He reached for the phone. "Dirk. What's up?" Hank turned his back to Amy and hung his legs over the edge of the bed.

"Chief Grey stopped by this morning to task us with a job. We're needed in Carbon County to back-up the deputies on a drug bust. How soon can you meet me at the Sheriff's Office?"

Hank's chest deflated as once again, he felt torn between his wife and his job. He ran a hand over his face and drew in a deep breath. "What time is it?" he asked as he held his phone out to look for himself. "Hold on a sec."

He glanced over his shoulder to find Amy glaring at him with her arms crossed over her chest. She had pulled on a robe and both the tightness of the cinched belt and the narrowed expression on her face told him his plan of spending the day in bed with her was no longer an option. Not that he could have said no to Dirk, but even if he had, it clearly wouldn't have mattered. He lost simply by answering Dirk's call.

He reached for his boxers. "I can be there in a little over an hour."

"Good. See you then." Dirk ended the call.

"So." Amy added a toe tap to her disapproval. "I can see nothing has changed while I was gone."

"That's not fair. Can we not throw out a wonderful night together just because I got a call from work?" Old frustration, hot and thick, clogged his throat.

"You're the one throwing us to the side to go running to Dirk. It's Sunday! Can't you even have one weekend off?"

"I'm always on call for my job. There aren't enough of us to cover multiple shifts. You know that. And Chief Grey will comp my day off later in the week. I'll get the time back. Why can't you be a little flexible? It seems like you want me to bend to your schedule, but you never have any room for mine."

Her eyes drew into slits. "I do nothing but accommodate your erratic schedule. Everything is about *your* job, and *your* friends. I'm sick of it!"

"That's not true." Even as he said the words, he realized she was right. But only because Amy didn't have a job or any friends of her own. Her entire focus was on getting pregnant. Maybe she wanted a baby so she wouldn't be alone during the day. He hoped not. That was a big burden to put on an infant. "Maybe it would help if you joined a club or took a class and made some friends you could connect with."

Amy's arms shot down to her sides, and her hands curled into fists. Her face went red. "Now it's *my* fault? Because I don't have friends to distract me from the fact that you're never home?"

He stood and splayed his fingers out as though he could stop the tirade that was coming. "That's not what I'm saying. I'm trying to problem solve."

"You're trying to sidetrack me from the point of this argument which is why do you always choose work over me?"

Minutes ticked by and Hank felt the pressure. He needed to shower and get dressed but he couldn't see a way to do that without making things worse. "Amy, I love you. And I have to go to work. Both things are true. Can we talk about this when I get home? Maybe we could take my day off this week and go somewhere together?"

"It won't make a difference."

He sighed. She was right. If she believed things wouldn't get better, then she'd inadvertently prevent his attempts. "Well, I hope you'll change your mind about that, but for now, I have to go."

"Long time, no see," Hank shook Dirk's hand when he entered the Carbon County Sheriff's Office. Hank came from Billings, but since Dirk had stayed the night at his cabin, his drive was shorter, and they met up in Red Lodge.

"Yeah. Sucks you had to come in on a Sunday. Is Amy pissed?"

He answered with a grim expression. "Last night was good for us, but it was a rough morning."

"Sorry about that."

Deputy Manning entered the reception area. "Thanks for coming guys. I really appreciate your help. Come on back to the office and we can strategize our approach for tonight."

Dirk shook his hand. "Where's the sheriff?"

"Out of town, I think visiting his sister. Come on back."

Hank followed Dirk and Manning to the back office where Olsen was staring at the topographical map, he had spread out flat on a desk.

Manning used his pen as a pointer. "Here's the outlay of the ranch where the deal is going to go down."

"Where did you get your intel?" Dirk asked without looking at their map. "We need more than just your gut feelings to go on."

Manning stammered under Sterling's intense gaze. Hank's shoulders tensed in empathy for the man. He'd experienced that armor-piercing glare himself and was glad to be on the opposite side of it this time.

"Uh, well. We have a guy on the inside."

"On the inside of what? Who are the players here?"

"Our informant works for the buyer. We brought him in on a drunk and disorderly and he told me a shipment was coming in tonight. He'd heard the deal was taking place at a ranch outside of town. But he admitted the location might change at the last minute if there is any hint of a security issue."

"How long have you worked with your CI? How well do you trust him?"

"I grew up with him. He went to jail on a drug charge when he was twenty-one. He got out five years later and that's when we tapped him. He's snitched for us several times since then. His information has been accurate so far. But there have been times that deals he told us about didn't happen. We have to accept that as part of the deal."

Hank glanced at Dirk to gauge his reaction. His partner nodded slowly and approached the desk. It looked like the stakeout was on, and a burst of adrenaline heated Hank's blood. They studied the map, reconnoitering it with the more familiar road atlas. The ranch in question sat deep inside a canyon.

"This location may make the dealers feel safe, but it gives us an ample selection of high positions to surveil them from." Hank pointed to several desirable spots.

Dirk tapped his finger on the one he liked the best. "How well do you shoot with a sniper rifle, Hank?"

"I shot Expert in the Army. But it's been a while."

Sterling smirked and swung his gaze toward him. "So pretty damn good, then?"

Hank shrugged. With his buddies, he'd have bragged about being a shit-hot shooter, but with Sterling, he would rather prove himself in action. "I had a lot of time to practice after I switched my MOS and became an MP. Where do you want me?"

Dirk's commanding presence took over the room. The sheriff's deputies were soon taking direction from him. It was his nature. Hank had seen that kind of instinctive leadership in the Service, and not always from the officer ranks. One of the most natural leaders he had ever known was a Crew Chief he flew with in his squadron. The man had died in Hank's helicopter crash. The country lost many top-quality men that day.

Hank bit the inside of his cheek bringing himself back to focus on the task at hand and away from the deep-seated pain of his memories. Dirk took a red pen and marked Hank's mission location. "I'll be on the ridge across the valley from you. Once they enter the canyon, we'll have them trapped."

Deputy Manning propped himself on the edge of the desk with both hands. "Where do you want us?"

"It's your show. We're just here to support you."

"Yeah, but what do you advise?"

Dirk scratched his chin. "You should be on the ground. How many people does your informant say will be there?"

"No more than six. He's part of a two-man crew and he thinks that the dealer's gang will have two or three."

"Thinks but doesn't know. Remember that."

Manning chewed his lip and tapped the map. "There's only one way into the canyon. I thought it would be good to wait till all the players show up and then block the road with a cruiser."

"You *could* do that, but we don't have enough manpower to leave anyone there to drive the vehicle. You two will have to be prepared to stop the deal. Which means you'll need to be in position before it happens. Hank and I will be posted on high ground ready for back-up in case anything goes sideways. We'll keep the comms open, so we know where each other are at all times."

Hank's nerves hummed with anticipation as he copied the coordinates of his designated location into his smart-watch. "We heading up now?"

Manning's eyes darted to him and then to Dirk. "It's not even noon, yet."

Hank took a photo of the map with his phone. "The sooner we get into position, the better. If I were a drug dealer, I'd probably send someone in early to run a site check. We need to be in place there before they arrive."

Sterling made coordinate calculations on his watch.

"I've got MRE's in my Jeep, if you're good with that, along with a bunch of extra gear we might need. We could be there all night."

Hank grinned. It had been a long time since he'd enjoyed the wonders of a military-style Meal Ready to Eat. "I dibs a spaghetti and meatballs if you have one. Those are the bomb!"

Dirk shook his head obviously doing his best not to grin. He kept a tight rein on his emotions and Hank made it a personal mission to break through Sterling's defenses. It was like winning a medal whenever he could get the man to crack a smile, let alone laugh.

"Are you men all set with a plan for your part of the raid?" Dirk asked the sheriff's deputies.

"Yes, sir. We'll be in place and will wait until the product and payment are in play. Then we'll move in."

"Good. Let's be vigilant out there."

CHAPTER 18

irk signaled to Hank and the two sheriff's deputies that he was in position. Hank responded that he too was at the ready. The deputies seemed competent, and Dirk hoped the bust would go smoothly. Small-town cops tended to have less experience in law enforcement but made up for it with the tracking and shooting skills they learned as kids growing up in the country.

It was two hours before sunset when Dirk opened his MRE. The pork patty meal was not his favorite. It was too salty, and the texture triggered his gag reflex but, in a pinch, it would do the trick. He'd given Hank his preference. Dirk had tried in the beginning to keep Flannigan at arm's length hoping to avoid the pain and grief he'd gone through when an explosion killed his previous partner. It was better not to get so close; not to be vulnerable. But the kid was worming his way under Dirk's skin, whether he liked it or not.

A black SUV traversed the serpentine gravel road that

passed by the road to the ranch. Dirk tapped his mic. "Vehicle approaching. Stay out of sight."

He followed the SUV with his binoculars as it slowed about fifty feet from the entrance. Instead of turning up the ranch road, the driver passed by and continued on. Dirk lost sight of the car when it drove beyond the ridge where he was perched. Five minutes later, it returned, traveling slower on the second pass. This time, the vehicle stopped at the ranch gate.

Dirk concentrated on slow breaths to keep his heart from racing. The SUV turned onto the drive and crawled toward the house. As the car got closer, he noticed it had no license plates. The driver circled around the home and barn before coming to a complete stop. Three armed men exited the car with their guns drawn and executed a property check.

One of the men dashed into the barn while the other two inspected the house. When they found no one, they returned to their car. Dirk checked his watch. One hour until sundown.

The car pulled forward stopping again fifty feet from the entry gate where two of the men riding in the back hopped out. They each made their way to opposite sides of the road and disappeared in the trees and scrub-like vegetation of the surrounding forest. All the activity he witnessed, along with the presence of the two lookouts, confirmed a deal was indeed happening that night.

"And that, gentlemen, is why we came out here hours before the transaction," Dirk murmured into the radio. "Flannigan, you and I will drop down and neutralize those two forward surveillance spotters."

"Roger that," came Hank's response.

Dirk checked the magazine in his Glock 19 out of habit. It was full, along with the round he kept in the chamber. He and Hank had camoed-up before they hiked into position, so Dirk was ready to creep down the hill and secure the scout on his side of the canyon.

The edge of the ridge was steep, and he did not relish the climb back up once he'd done his job below. He traversed his way approximately halfway down the two-hundred-foot slope when his boots slipped from under him. His body shot straight down a rolling rockslide like an arrow. Stones tumbled before him, launching off a cliff edge below.

Dirk had no way of knowing how far he'd fall if he flew off the ledge behind the loose rocks. The topographical map had given him the grade of incline, but he hadn't realized there was a drop-off. Desperately, he searched for a way to stop his momentum. Scrambling with all his strength, Dirk rolled to his side and fought to swim upstream of the dirt and rock cascading around him.

His elbow struck the trunk of a small pine tree at the edge of the slide. It scraped the skin up the length of his arm as he slid by, and at the last second, Dirk grabbed hold of the tree and stopped his desent. Hanging from one arm, he flung his other hand up to get a better grip and pull himself out of danger.

The spotter below had to have heard the noise, which made taking him down that much more dangerous. Dirk sucked in lungs full of air infused with the stringent scent of crushed wild sage and pine. He low crawled to a nearby rock outcropping, pausing just long enough to catch his breath before maneuvering laterally across the slope.

Finally, descending further until he landed at the same elevation as his prey.

He spotted the scout, and relief flooded through him. The guy wore earbuds in his ears and was smoking a cigarette—none the wiser to Dirk's fall that should have announced his presence. He crept toward the spotter and positioned himself behind the boulder against which the man leaned, tapping his toes to his music. Silently, Dirk sprang, knocking the lookout off his feet. He threw his arm around the man's neck placing him in a choke hold and held tight.

With the help of a high dose of oxygen-sucking adrenaline, the scout passed out fast and Dirk released him to the ground. He bound the unconscious man's hands and feet with duct tape, and stuffed a wad of gauze in his mouth, taping over his lips and around his head three times. With a length of rope, he secured his captive to a tree so he couldn't go anywhere once he came to.

"I'll be back to get you, don't worry," Dirk whispered to the comatose man. As fast as he could, Dirk assessed the scrape on his arm. No immediate care was necessary, so he started up the mountain the way he had come, this time avoiding the treacherous cliff.

CHAPTER 19

Sunset came and went, and the night air cooled. It was 2:30 am when Dirk last checked his watch. He tapped his mic and whispered, "Comm check."

"Dash two, check."

"Three, check."

"Dash four."

"Stay alert, boys. We know they're coming *sometime*."

Thirty-five minutes later, an old farm truck bounced along the moonlit road. It stopped before turning onto the ranch drive. Dirk's body thrummed with anticipation and his mind clicked into full alert.

The old Ford crawled up the long drive with country music blaring from its open windows. After circling around, it came to a stop with the headlights beaming toward the entrance gate. Two occupants exited the vehicle, leaving the doors of the cab open like wings.

One man climbed into the bed of the truck while the other ran to the barn and switched on powerful floodlights that brought the light of day to the barnyard. Dirk peered through his binoculars to confirm there were only two men in this phase of the deal.

Manning's voice filled Dirk's ear. "The guy who just lit up the place is our informant. Don't shoot him."

"Roger that." *He won't get shot so long as he doesn't start shooting at us first.* You could only trust an informant as far as their last stint in jail.

The black SUV from earlier returned, driving at a snail's pace. It turned up the ranch road and stopped thirty feet in front of the truck. The vehicles stood head-to-head. All four doors of the black vehicle opened. Three men and a woman stepped out, armed to the gills. The sellers had arrived.

Dirk watched the scene unfold through the scope on his service-issued Colt M4 Carbine. The tinted windows on the SUV prevented Dirk from seeing if anyone else remained inside the vehicle when the dealers carried a hard-sided case out to the middle ground. The buyers approached the chest to sample the merchandise.

This was no high-powered deal. The unprofessional buyer punctured the brick of white powder with a pocketknife and drew out a hit. He snorted the cocaine straight from the blade. Idiot. Who knew what they had cut into that powder. Even a tiny amount of fentanyl could be deadly. Lucky for him the snort didn't kill the guy instantly. He and his partner grinned like kids at Christmas and Dirk figured they'd end up getting themselves killed, anyway.

The informant ran back to the truck for the money. He slowed down as he returned to the middle ground with a duffle bag and opened it to show the dealers the cash. All players moved toward the money like bears to honey.

"Police! Drop your weapons. Put your hands over your heads!" Manning yelled from the shadows below.

Dirk prayed the deputy had sufficient cover because as the dealers dropped to their knees, they fired a barrage of bullets toward the sound of his voice. The CI and his cohort dove behind their truck to avoid being shot. With no discernible rifle report, the drug dealer closest to Manning's position fell forward. The delayed boom sounded a split-second after the target crumpled—his face striking the ground. Hank had dropped his first long-range target.

Dirk steadied his aim and releasing his breath, he squeezed the trigger, and took down the man shooting from the back of the pack. The other two dealers, realizing they were outgunned, dropped their weapons, and raised their hands over their heads.

Before the situation was fully secured, the second sheriff's deputy left his position to apprehend them. Dirk's heart kicked in his chest as he helplessly watched the scene unfold. One of the buyers grabbed his weapon, leveled it, and fired. As if in slow motion, Dirk shot his rifle again, taking the shooter out. But not before the deputy dropped to the ground.

"Officer down!" Dirk yelled. No longer worried about hiding his presence.

He ran from his position across the ridge carefully avoiding the loose rocks. Pine branches scratched his face as he flew down the hill toward the ranch. Yanking the sat phone from his tactical vest he called for emergency services. "Officer down. I repeat, Officer down!" he yelled as he ran dodging trees and leaping over rocks.

Hank beat him to the scene and held the two remaining criminals and the informant at gunpoint while Manning secured their weapons and cuffed their hands behind their backs. Dirk paused to confirm the SUV was empty before he raced to assist the fallen officer. He darted across the drive and dropped, skidding on his knees to a stop by the deputy's side.

Dirk assessed the amount of blood the young lawman had lost, and unbuckled his belt, sliding it from his hips. Manning finished securing the drug dealers and then yanked off his coat and pressed it against his partner's leg.

"Give me some room," Dirk said as he tightened his belt around the deputy's thigh, using the leather cinch as a tourniquet. "Hang on, buddy. Help is on the way."

CHAPTER 20

Beaux threw his juice glass against the wall. Following the crash of broken glass, orange liquid ran down the wallpaper in shard-filled rivulets and pooled on the floor. "What the hell happened? That deal should have gone through as smooth as velvet. Everything was in place." In his fury, he swept the toaster, a crockery container filled with various kitchen utensils, and the salt and pepper shakers sending them sailing off the kitchen counter onto the floor. His robe flew open, and he tugged it back over his large belly hiding the rounded bulge drooping over the waistband of his boxers.

"I don't know, boss. Somehow the cops were on to it." Troy pointed to the mess on the tile. "Rufus, clean that up."

"The *cops*? What cops? There's only the Carbon County deputies and they certainly aren't up to organizing a take-down like that." Beaux's heated face throbbed in time with his pulse. A bust like this could ruin his infant business. Someone on the inside was a weasel. It was the only expla-nation. "What happened to all my dope? God damn it! I needed that merchandise to start the narcotics side of my business."

Troy opened the refrigerator to avoid eye contact with him and Rufus kept his head down as he wiped up the juice and glass mess.

"Another thing to think about, boss."

"What?" Beaux was not in the mood for more problems.

"We're going to have to find a new stooge to launder the drug money now that Molly is... being used for other things. But it might be good to lie low for a little while. Until things cool down."

"*Good* to lie low? Do you know how much cash I've laid down? Money that is currently in the evidence locker at the Sheriff's Office?"

Ted wandered into the kitchen. "Is there any coffee left?" He stopped when he noticed the broken glass, and he took in the mess around the room. He looked at each man's face, finally landing on Beaux's. "What were you saying about the Sheriff's Office?"

Troy filled him in on the thwarted drug deal the night before. "And now the boss is out both the coke and the cash."

"I don't believe it. Let me make some calls." The first place he dialed was the Carbon County Sheriff's Department. He spoke with the receptionist. When he ended the call, he slammed his phone onto the counter. "Deputy Manning arrested five suspects last night. Two of our team members were killed, and one is in critical condition. A deputy was shot in the leg and is recovering from surgery at a hospital in Bozeman and one of our men is in ICU, under guard, at the same hospital. The deputy in charge isn't at the office because he's currently eating breakfast at a diner in Red Lodge, happy as you please. And get this. He's there with those two Deputy US Marshals who've been poking their noses in all around the county. What the hell happened last night?"

"That's what I want to know. You're the man responsible for avoiding messes like this, and you'd better fix it." Beaux's seething anger refused to cool. "You need to get my cash *and* that smack out of the evidence locker, *today*. And take care of the idiot in ICU. We can't have him talking while he's medicated. Do you understand me?"

"That'll be impossible…"

"Are you talking to me? I can't hear you unless you are saying 'Yes, sir.'" Beaux choked on his anger and strode from the kitchen. This was Molly's doing. It had to be. How else would the deputy marshals have heard about the deal? She was going to pay dearly for her disloyalty. A sin Beaux would never forgive. He stormed down the hallway to find her. He planned to take all his fury out on that bitch. Right. Now.

When he arrived at the set of rooms where they kept the children and Molly, the guard he'd posted unlocked the door and let him in. He scanned the room. Plenty of delectable options for the choosing, but this time he sought one person in particular as the canvas for his rage.

"Molly!" he yelled. The children cowered, many of them hiding their faces as if they couldn't see him, then he couldn't see them either. Foolish little things. Molly did not appear at his summons. Blood coursed through him like lava and his fury tinted the room red.

Beaux snatched a small girl by her hair and dragged her alongside him as he stomped toward the adjoining room. "Molly, you'd better show yourself front and center, or I'm going to use this kid to rid me of the anger I feel toward you!"

The little girl whimpered, and other children cried with her in sympathy. The wailing effect was successful. Molly stepped out from behind the shower curtain in the Jack-and-Jill bathroom where she'd been doing her hair.

"I'm here." Her voice was so small he could hardly hear her words.

Beaux shoved the girl to the side, and she fell to the floor. In two strides he towered over Molly and back-handed her across the mouth. Her lip split and she flew against the sink bruising her hip bone. She cried out until he grabbed her by the throat and pushed her against the wall. She sputtered for air. Her face turned maroon, then purple. Her eyes bugged.

"What did you tell those marshals?"

She clutched at his hands, tearing at his fingers, and shook her head. He eased his grip slightly to allow her to speak.

"I didn't—"

He released her neck and threw a punch. He was not about to listen to her lies and excuses. "Tell me what you said to them! You cost me over five-hundred grand, you stupid bitch!"

Molly covered her battered face and slid down the wall. Beaux yanked her up to her feet by her arm and then grabbing the collar of her shirt, he tore the garment from her body.

"No! Johnny! Not here. Not in front of the children." Her eyes were wild as she tried to cover herself. Her desperate fear inflamed his excitement. His body hardened.

He took hold of the hot curling iron on the counter and yanked its cord from the wall. "My name is not Johnny, you ignorant whore." He laughed with menace. "And I'll do what I please to you, when and where I want to do it. Besides, it's better if these brats know what's coming for them." He pulled her arms away from her chest and dragged her across the room. He threw her onto the bed. When she cried out, he whipped her with the electrical cord. Each time she denied him, she paid for it either with a whip or skin-sizzling burn, increasing his pleasure, until she finally lay dazed, whimpering, and fully compliant.

Beaux was vaguely aware of the kids cowering in the other room. He didn't care. He'd seen men use his own mother in this same way when he was their age. Sometimes they forced him to watch, which at first horrified him and made him cry. But eventually, he grew numb to the abuse, and *he* turned out just fine. Even when those same men came after him, raping him, too. He had hated it. Hated everything about those men. But he learned from them too. He learned how to make money and the crucial knowledge that with great money came incredible power.

He took what he wanted from Molly and left her in a bloody, sticky, mess on the rumpled sheets. This was the way he had learned about life when he was a kid, and again at the group home where he'd lived after his mother died. And it was the same way these kids would learn to survive. Hell, in a way, he was doing them a favor.

CHAPTER 21

Life Flight arrived just before dawn and flew the injured deputy along with the drug dealing suspect to a hospital in Bozeman. Afterward, state investigators took over the crime scene. Remorse squeezed Dirk's chest, and he avoided looking at the dead bodies lying in the dirt near the SUV while he and Hank helped Deputy Manning gather the two lookout men, the remaining dealer, the buyer, and the informant. Splitting them between their two cars, they took the suspects to jail. They left the scene in the capable hands of the state investigators. Once the dirtbags were processed and locked away, the lawmen drove to the nearby diner for much needed coffee, breakfast, and a debrief.

"I can't thank you guys enough for backing us up." Manning took a steaming sip. "No way could we have handled that on our own."

Dirk took a long sip of hot coffee and rubbed his morning beard. "Not a problem. I just hope your partner is going to be okay. He lost situational awareness and left his cover, but the second buyer was still armed." He shook his head with regret.

Hank swallowed a bite of eggs. "Yeah. It's too bad too because Dirk had to shoot the guy. He could have given us information on who they worked for. Hopefully, the cops can get the guy in the hospital to give up some intel."

Dirk's phone buzzed. "It's the chief. I gotta take this." He turned away from them in his seat. "Good morning."

"I'm glad to hear your voice. You forgot to call me with your SIT REP last night."

"Sorry, I never had the opportunity. We just now sat down for a cup of coffee and some food. What time is it?" Dirk glanced at his watch as he asked.

"It's ten. How'd it go? You and Henry are both safe? Did you shut down the deal?"

"Yeah, but it wasn't an ideal op. We ended up arresting four of the six players on the dealer's side and both buyers, but one of them is an informant. Deputy Olsen and one of the suspects had to be airlifted to the hospital. Olsen had emergency surgery on his leg, and the injured suspect is under guard in ICU. Two of their crew did not survive the event."

"Is Olsen going to be alright?"

"I don't know. He lost a lot of blood."

"I'll call the hospital for an update. Were you able to connect the drugs to Crandall?"

"Not yet. So far, the dealers, who we suspect are working for Crandall, aren't talking, and neither is the buyer." Dirk's eyes were gritty—burning when he blinked —and his chest ached. "I'm sick about Olsen getting shot. The kid just ran out, Em. He left his cover, and I was a split second too late in taking down the shooter."

Gentle compassion wove through Emory's voice and soothed his raw emotions. "Olsen's injuries are not your fault, Dirk. He should have kept his cover."

"I know, but he's so young."

"I'll keep you posted with any news from the hospital, and I want a full report from you guys by the end of the day."

"Any chance you'd give us until tomorrow? We were up all night, and I don't think Hank got any sleep the night before that." Dirk's body hurt. The weight of his exhaustion and sense of guilt pressed heavily on his shoulders. All he wanted was a hot shower and his bed. "We're debriefing with Deputy Manning now, and then Hank and I will head back to Billings."

"That's fine."

Dirk barely registered the door of the diner swinging open as he breathed in the rich, hot steam rising from his mug. Sheriff Donnelly marched across the room toward their table. His furious expression had Dirk rising to his feet. "Hey, Chief, I gotta go. I'll call you when I get home." He clicked off.

"Manning! Just what in the hell did you think you were doing last night? I never gave you clearance for any joint missions with the US Marshal Service!" Sheriff Donnelly spat his words in anger.

"Uh, well, sir, I tried to reach you. I had solid intel that a deal was going down, so I called the marshals in for support."

"I never got a message from you on my phone." The sheriff jabbed and scrolled on his device's screen.

"I didn't leave one because I hung up and tried to radio your cruiser, instead."

"I had to coordinate with the FBI to find those missing kids and then I went to my sister's house. I was not in my cruiser. Damn it, Manning! You don't have the authority to call in the marshals or to go on a takedown on your own. Now Deputy Olsen is fighting for his life, and it's your fault."

Manning shrank in his seat at the accusation. "We stopped the drug deal, confiscated the drugs *and* the money, and have four of the suspects in jail."

"And your partner might die in the process. Was it worth it?" Red faced; the sheriff jammed his hands onto his hips.

"Sheriff," Dirk stepped in. "Manning did everything by the book. Olsen got shot because he left his cover too soon. Other than that, it was a good bust."

Donnelly's glare swung to Dirk. "He had no business acting on the CI's information without my say-so."

"You were nowhere to be found." Dirk was in no mood for the blame game. "By the way, why didn't you answer your phone? Manning tried calling you several times."

The man's face deepened to an eggplant hue. "I don't answer to you, Deputy Marshal Sterling."

"No. And I don't answer to you either. It was a good bust, and I'd think you would want to congratulate your sharp deputy rather than berate him."

The sheriff bunched himself up to say something, but then thought better of it. He turned back to Manning. "From now on, you do not make a move without my prior approval. Do you understand me? You're one signature away from losing your job."

Manning stared at his pancakes. "Yes, sir."

The sheriff stormed from the dinner, and Dirk returned to his seat. "What a jackass."

Hank sopped up the few scraps of food left on his plate with a buttered slice of toast. "I don't know why he's so pissed. The raid is a feather in the cap of his department."

The server topped off their cups with hot coffee. Manning thanked her, then said, "He's probably mad because he can't take credit for it."

"Maybe." Dirk wasn't so sure. Something was off. Why would a sheriff be angry about his deputies stopping a major drug deal in their county? There had to more to it than simple hurt pride.

Two men entered the diner and sat on stools at the counter. They looked vaguely familiar, but Dirk couldn't place them. "Hey, Bella," the taller one called to the server.

"Hold your horses, I'm coming. Just getting a fresh pot." Bella exchanged the almost empty coffee carafe for a freshly brewed one and leaned against the counter to pour. "What can I get you fellas this morning?"

"Coffee's good. Listen, have you seen Molly?"

"Molly Briggs? From over in Edgar? No, why?"

Dirk eavesdropped on the conversation while he dug into the second half of his breakfast burrito.

"She said she would try to take my lunch shift at the bar today, but I can't get ahold of her. I tried to call her all last night and this morning. I want to go fishing, but if I'm not there and nobody shows up to cover me, I'll lose my job."

"If she said she'd do it, she will. You know Molly. She never lets anyone down."

"But she only said, maybe."

Bella shrugged and made a trip around the restaurant

with her fresh pot. Hank held up his cup when she came to their table.

"You better slow down, honey. You'll be jittery all day," Bella teased Hank as she filled his mug to the brim.

"Sorry for listening in, Bella." Dirk nudged his cup toward her. "But is it normal for Molly not to answer her phone?"

"No." She chuckled. "That girl is attached to that thing like it's a permanent body part."

"Why do you think she didn't answer that guy's calls, then?"

"I can't say. She really isn't the type to leave a friend hanging. It is strange—I hope she's alright. Maybe I should run by her place after I get off." Bella's brow furrowed as she checked her watch. "'Course, that won't be 'till after Donny's lunch shift starts. And Edgar is a good forty minutes up the road."

"We could run by and check on her for you on our way back to Billings, if you want." Hank and Manning both turned their attention toward Dirk, suddenly interested in the conversation.

"Would you? That'd be so sweet." She patted his shoulder. "Deputy Manning, you know where Molly lives, don't you?"

"Yep, I'll get them her address."

"You boys are awful sweet. Coffee's on the house this morning." She smiled down at them before she made her way to the next table.

"What's on your mind?" Hank glanced at Dirk as he stirred cream and sugar into his mug.

"Nothing, really. Just a gut feeling. I'll rest easier when we find Molly and make sure she's safe. From the sound of it, she's expected at the bar for the lunch service. It's ten-thirty, now."

"The bar opens at eleven-thirty for lunch," Manning added. "She'd probably be there by now if she's working."

"Good. We'll start there."

CHAPTER 22

On their way to the bar in Edgar, Hank got a text from Amy. **When will you be home?**

Hank: **Not sure.**

Amy: **You never texted to let me know you were safe.**

Hank: **Sorry, babe. We've been busy.**

Amy: **I see.**

Hank felt the disappointment and the accusation through the typed words. He pressed his head back against the seat and closed his eyes.

"Everything okay?" Dirk asked.

"Yeah. It's just Amy checking in."

Dirk side-eyed him but didn't comment.

Amy: **R U still there?**

Hank: **Yeah**

Amy: **Today is a good day for - you know. We still have a couple hours… if you care.**

He couldn't keep up with the switch-back trail of her emotions. It was nearly impossible to be patient with her, even though he understood a lot of the drama had to do with the hormones her doctor had her on.

Hank: **Of course, I care, Amy. We've gotta do something in Edgar and then we'll be home. But I'm exhausted. I haven't slept in the past two nights.**

Amy: **I just need 5 minutes of your precious time and energy.**

Hank clicked his phone off and closed his eyes. He had thought things were getting a little better, but then they fought again before he left. Amy was still singularly focused and pissed if he didn't jump up and perform.

"Mid-day booty call?" Dirk chuckled.

Hank forced a smile but couldn't fake more than that. "Something like that."

"Most guys would love that."

"Probably."

"We'll just stop in at the bar and then head back to Billings. We'll be there in about an hour, tops."

"Good. I'm beat."

Dirk was silent the rest of the way, and Hank was glad. He was too tired to talk. When they parked, Dirk made no move to open the door of the SUV. "How old are you?"

"Twenty-seven. Why?"

"Why aren't you racing to get home? You've got a beautiful wife who wants you, man. Don't take that for granted."

Hank pressed his eyes closed with his thumb and middle finger. "The thing is it isn't *me* she wants. She just needs me to perform the act."

"And you're complaining because…"

"Never mind." Hank reached for the door handle. He

didn't need any shit from Sterling. He got way more than enough of that at home, from Amy.

"Hey, kid. Hold up."

"What?" He released his grip on the lever, and it snapped back.

"I don't know what you're going through. And I don't need to know. But you need to work it out because when you're on the job you need total focus. Otherwise, you could get yourself killed." Dirk paused and smirked. "Or worse—me."

"I know." Hank flopped his head against the headrest. "I thought we *had* worked it out. Amy went to her mom's for a while and then after dinner at your place, she came back home. We had a great night, but then she got mad that I had to go to work and now the demands for the dog and pony show have started up again. You'd think an all-nighter with her would be enough." Hank pushed his door open. He was sure he'd already said more than Sterling wanted to hear. "Don't worry. We'll figure it out."

Dirk grabbed the handle on the flaking red door of the bar, but he didn't pull it open. "You can talk to me if you want to, you know. I hear partners do that sometimes." He clapped Hank on the back and yanked open the door, holding it for him to go through.

The early liquid-lunch crowd was already in place, only Molly was not behind the bar. The bartender was the same man who had asked Bella about Molly at the diner. Hank and Dirk sat on stools at the end of the bar and waited for the guy to come over.

"What can I get for you guys?"

"My friend here will have a Pepsi since he's not old enough to drink. I'll have coffee."

Hank chuckled despite his pissy mood. When the bartender returned with their drinks, he asked if they wanted any food.

Dirk rotated his coffee mug around and gripped the handle. "No, thanks. We actually stopped by because we're concerned about Molly. Any idea where she is?"

The man screwed his lips together and frowned. "No. If I knew where she was, I wouldn't be here. Why? Who's asking?"

"We're friends of hers. We overheard you talking to Bella at the diner in Red Lodge and now we're wondering if she's okay."

The bartender polished a wineglass. "You think she's sick or something?"

"Yeah. It's not like her to play hooky from work. Is it?"

"No. But maybe she just forgot. This isn't her usual shift. She was doing me a favor. She probably went out last night and is hungover or something. I didn't check her house."

Hank gulped his soda thankful for the cold, sweet caffeine. "We could run by and see if she's there."

"That'd be great. If she's home, I could still get to the river. If she gets here in the next hour, anyway."

"What's the best way to drive to her house from here?"

"I thought you were her friends?"

Dirk sipped his coffee and added cream. "We are, but we've never been to her place."

"It's the last house at the end of Montana Street. Three streets north from here."

The town was only a few blocks long, so they didn't ask for further directions. "We'll call the bar if we find her." Dirk wrote his phone number on a napkin. "Do the same for us if you hear from her. Will you?"

"Yeah, sure."

They left what remained of their drinks and drove to Molly's. It was a tiny house made of cinderblocks. Once painted white, it was now a dingy gray. The sparse yard was a section of gravel and weeds.

They went to the front and Hank knocked on the flimsy aluminum screen-door. No one answered, not even a dog. Dirk peered in through the front window and shook his head.

"I'll check the back." Hank walked around the house to what he presumed was the kitchen door. No one answered there, either. He met Dirk at the SUV.

"There's not a lot of places she could be in this pit stop of a town." Dirk slid back into the car. "But she might have gone somewhere else. Maybe she's visiting relatives or something." He started the engine. "But I've got a bad feeling. Something's off. We can call the bar tomorrow and see if she ever turned up, but for now, let's get you home."

Hank was definitely looking forward to his bed. Just not with the demands attached to it.

———

Emory didn't expect to see Dirk or Henry until the following day. They hadn't slept all night due to the coordinated drug bust in Carbon County. At first, she had thought Dirk making a connection between Beaux Crandall and the sudden up-spurt of drug and gun deals going down in the Montana area was far-fetched, but she was learning to trust his intuition more and more. She spent the morning looking deeper into Crandall's history to see if she could find anything else that pointed to his presence in Montana.

She dug into the arrest reports from Louisiana and followed Crandall's illegal tracks back as far as she could until she came to the sealed documents from when he was a minor. The fact that there were sealed court records told her enough. The man had lived a life full of violence and crime since he was a kid. He had been accused of rape on more than one occasion but had never been convicted. He had two counts of aggravated assault and one for possession of child pornography. With each charge, he either pled out, or did only a fraction of his sentence. The charges against him at the hearing before he disappeared were money laundering, the sale of illegal firearms, and distribution of child pornography, and it looked like the prosecutor was finally going to get him. That's when he jumped his bail and disappeared—becoming a fugitive on the run.

If Dirk was right and Crandall had reappeared in their district, she was determined to catch him. Next, she accessed the few files she could find from the time Crandall spent in foster care as a child. Child and Family Services removed him from his home after the court convicted his mother of child abuse and the sale of her son into prostitution. His father had died a year earlier of a drug overdose.

Emory let out a long breath. "This kind of start in life would screw anybody up," she murmured to herself as she made a note of the caseworker's name and the number of the agency on a bright orange sticky note. Maybe the woman was still working in Social Services, but she doubted it. The system pretty much chewed up social workers, burned them to ash, and spit them out. It was a low-paying, thankless job. One to which only saints need apply.

Her cell phone rang, and she smiled when she saw it was Dirk. "Hey, are you home?"

"On my way. I just left Hank at his house and thought I might grab a burger before I go home and hit the rack. Want to meet me? I can fill you in on our morning."

Emory glanced at her watch. Dave had left a message asking her to lunch, but she hadn't yet responded. She'd message him and tell him she wasn't available. Lunch with Dirk was a higher priority. It was imperative that they discuss their case. She ignored the flutter of anticipation in her belly, insisting to herself it was merely hunger pangs. "Sounds good." "Great. How about the Burger Dive in ten minutes?"

"I'll be there." Emory shot Dave a text. It was the coward's way out, but much easier than having to explain that she was choosing Dirk over him… again.

CHAPTER 23

Dirk hit the rack early and was awake before five the next morning. He'd dreamt of Molly crying out for help and he woke feeling frustrated and ill at ease. His brain was probably on overdrive after the adrenaline dump from the night before. He made himself a strong pot of coffee and after his first cup, took a long, hot shower. For the last two minutes, he blasted his body with cold water. His every muscle tensed, but the cold gave him the acute clarity of mind he needed.

With a second cup of joe in hand, Dirk padded out to the deck with his laptop. He took a few minutes enjoying the view of the distant mountains before he followed up on the information Emory shared with him the day before. Crandall had suffered physical and sexual abuse as a child before he entered the foster care system in Louisiana. He ended up living in a group home that was shut down when Crandall was fourteen due to allegations of child abuse and neglect. After that, he found no further record of Crandall until he turned eighteen. The first official record he discovered was one for an arrest. He'd been accused of raping a minor, but they dismissed the case for lack of evidence.

Dirk read the court filings. The documents did not reveal the accuser's identity. Her name was redacted because of her age—only twelve. Dirk swiped his hand over his face. This Crandall dude was screwed up. How had he gone from an abused kid with no future, to the crime kingpin he had become before he disappeared in Louisiana?

According to Dirk's research, the guy would have been fifty-nine when he was arrested. The *Chicago Tribune* reported him to be worth millions at the time of his arraignment. He must have gotten one hell of an education from the streets. When the police arrested him for the final time in Natchitoches Parish, it was for dealing in high-dollar drugs, weapons, and child pornography.

Dirk checked his watch. It was still too early to call, but he wanted to talk to the arresting officer and to the DA who handled Crandall's case. The recent drug and gun deals they'd uncovered had Crandall's style all over them. Especially when Dirk considered the two dead men found with notes nailed to their heads. That took a particular sort of evil. The kind you might see in a homicidal sociopath.

Finally, it was time to go to work, and Dirk chose to drive his Jeep Rubicon. Even though it was the perfect morning for a ride, he had a feeling he and Hank would be driving back to Edgar. He arrived at the office half an hour early, and Emory was already there. *Did the woman ever go home?*

She was staring at her computer so deep in concentration she didn't notice him come in. He took advantage of the opportunity to watch her in the unguarded moment. Her hair on one side of her head was mussed, most likely from her habit of shoving it behind her ear while she read. She held a pencil in her teeth, alternately studying the screen and typing.

Emory paused for a moment and reached for her coffee cup. She glimpsed him standing outside her office and jumped, spilling hot brown liquid all over her desk. "Dirk! What are you doing, lurking around over there? You scared the crap out of me!" She snatched a handful of tissues and blotted up the mess.

"I'm sorry, but I wasn't lurking." *Liar,* he thought. "I just arrived. Have you been here all night?"

"No. But I couldn't sleep so I thought I'd come in and get some work done."

"I didn't sleep much either." He moved to his desk and turned on the computer. He raised his voice over his shoulder. "I had some weird dreams about the bartender in Edgar. She was screaming for help, but I couldn't find her."

"Did she ever turn up, yesterday?" Emory came out to the bullpen and perched her lovely backside on the edge of his desk. Her spicy cologne drifted under his nose, distracting him further.

He dragged his attention back to the conversation. "I don't know. I'll wait until eleven, which is when the bar opens, then I'll call over there and check in on her." Dirk took in the pensive expression on Emory's face and had the urge to smooth away the crease between her eyes. Instead, he flipped through a stack of mail. "I read all the official reports on Crandall. I can't believe he's avoided jail for as long as he has."

"Makes you wonder what judges he has in his pocket."

"No kidding."

"What happens if Molly's not at work?"

"Then Hank and I will run over to Edgar and put the squeeze on some locals. Maybe get the sheriff to open a missing persons investigation."

"She might turn up."

"Let's hope. But I left my number at the bar. No one has called so far."

Teresa and Hank arrived at the same time, just after eight. Hank's hair did not flip up in its usual impish swirl. Instead, it looked like he'd run his hand through his blond waves in a failed attempt to get them to lie down. Purple smudges pooled under his eyes and his ever-present smile was on vacation.

Dirk spun around in his chair to face him. "Rough night?"

"You could say that. I got only a little bit of sleep." Hank slumped into his chair.

Teresa gave Dirk google eyes and then rolled them when Hank's back was turned. Then taking pity on the kid, she asked, "Want a cup of coffee, Flannigan? I'm on my way to the kitchen."

"That'd be great." He rubbed his eyes and asked Dirk, "Any word from Molly?"

Dirk shook his head. "Not yet. We'll probably have to drive over there, later. You up for it?"

Hank closed his eyes but gave him the thumbs up.

"You can snooze on the way there, Sleeping Beauty."

"If that's the case, do you mind if I go wait in the car for you now?" Hank let out an exhausted chuff and rested his head against the back of his chair.

At 11:00 am, Dirk called the bar in Edgar and got the answer he expected but didn't want to hear. "No, I still haven't heard from her. She missed her shift last night, too. I drove by her place this morning, but she is nowhere to be seen."

"Have you reported her missing to the sheriff?"

"No. I'm reporting it to you. Hey, I gotta go. Lunch rush is coming in."

Dirk stood and stretched. "Come on kid, grab your go bag. We're going back over to Edgar."

Hank slept soundly on the drive, snoring softly. Dirk didn't wake him when he stopped at Molly's. He knocked, but the house was empty as reported, so he drove to the Sheriff's Department where he left Hank in the car once again. The kid was beat.

"Hey, Sterling." Deputy Manning stood when he walked in. "What brings you back down here so soon?"

"Remember yesterday morning at the diner when that guy came in and asked Bella if she'd seen Molly around?"

"Yeah?"

"Molly is still missing. I thought I'd talk to Donnelly and see if he's seen her anywhere. If not, you should open a missing persons investigation."

"Sheriff's not here. Haven't seen him since yesterday at the diner. But I can help you with the missing person's report."

"Where is he this time?"

"I don't know. I've been told too many times that he doesn't answer to me, so I quit asking."

"Sounds to me like you basically run the department and he's just the figurehead. You ever thought of running for Sheriff next time around?"

"I've considered it." Manning hid his shy grin in the stack of bins. He pulled a form out of a folder. "Fill this out with all the information you know about the missing woman."

Dirk chose a pen from a cup crammed full of pens and pencils. He tapped the point on the counter. Something odd was going on. Both Molly and the sheriff were missing. Dirk didn't buy into the idea of coincidences. "Is Sheriff Donnelly driving his cruiser, today?"

"I guess so. It's not here."

"It has a GPS tracker, doesn't it?"

"All our vehicles do. You know, in case we get stuck somewhere or something."

"Yeah." With some effort, Dirk kept the 'duh' out of his tone. Manning was a good guy even if he was a little slow on the uptake at times. "So, let's track him. I'd like to find him and bring him into the loop."

"I'm not supposed to track him without a solid reason."

"You can tell him *I* was worried about him. Let's do it."

Manning led Dirk to his computer and brought up the GPS map. Within seconds, a red location pointer flashed on the screen.

Dirk leaned over Manning's shoulder for a closer view. "Where is that? It looks like he's out in the middle of nowhere."

Manning zoomed in. "Looks like he's driving out Willow Creek Road. Maybe he's going out to see his sister, again. He won't like me looking into his personal business."

"Give me his number. I want to know what he's doing out there."

"Are you *trying* to get me in trouble, Sterling? I'm already in enough shit as it is after that unapproved raid on the drug deal we busted."

"Manning, does it strike you as odd, at all, that the sheriff was so angry about a successful bust?"

"Not really. He's always pissed about something."

Dirk set his jaw. "Something's going on, and I'm going to find out what it is." He took a screenshot of the map on Manning's computer.

CHAPTER 24

Beaux took a break for lunch. They'd been filming all morning, and he was getting weary of all the crying and wailing. Eventually, his little actors would give in and accept their fate in life. Video recording would be much easier, then. Of course, there was an audience that paid big dollars to watch the terror, pain, and tears, too. He made a mental note to highlight those features in a new line of marketing as he told his personal chef that he'd wait for his meal on the deck.

He poured himself a tall glass of iced tea and eased into a lounge chair. His view of the Beartooth Mountain Range was spectacular. Hummingbirds swooped up high with their green, gold, and magenta colors reflecting the sun. Then they dove straight down, their wings whistling with their speed, amazing him each time they missed crashing into the ground. He drew in the fresh air, and a delightful calmness filled his body. Nature brought with it a rare peace, but it didn't pay the bills. Beaux returned his mind to making more money.

Molly was proving to be useless with the kids. She flat-out refused to play a part in his scripts with them. He'd already filmed her regular discipline enough times. Troy had beaten and raped her within inches of her life, and the films were selling like cotton candy at the county fair. The only thing that was left to film now was her death. Troy would do it. He'd enjoy it in fact, so long as they blurred out his face. Real-life murder scenes brought in top dollar especially if you told a good story along with the act.

They could create a scene out in the barn. Maybe chain Molly to a stall door... or dangle her naked from the rafters after chasing her through the woods. He'd brainstorm with Troy after lunch and let the man do what he pleased. He'd earned it.

Beaux fantasized about doing the job himself for a few minutes, and the idea thrilled him more than he'd expected. But the risk was too great. He couldn't afford to be seen in any of the photos or videos he sold. Not with the feds biting at his heels all the time. He'd simply have to enjoy the act vicariously like his customers did. Except with one major difference. In his case, he'd have a live, front-row view of the event.

Snuff films were a hot commodity on the dark web, and though they didn't perform as well overall as the porn did, they sold for a higher price and made for a flourishing income stream. Of course, once your product was dead, it had to be replaced. That was costly and dangerous. He'd have to evaluate if the risk was worth the value. The best part of using children was you could sell them over and over as they grew up. A truly renewable resource.

The chef opened the French doors leading out to the deck, and Beaux's belly rolled in anticipation as the scent of the thick, five-cheese grilled sourdough sandwich reached his nose. He lifted the artisan bread dripping with melted cheddar and dunked it into a bowl of freshly made tomato soup. He groaned in pleasure at the blend of the tangy rich flavors.

Carrying his own tray, Troy joined him on the deck. "Nice day. Maybe we should film out here today—title it 'Afternoon Delight.'"

"I like your thinking."

"We could let the children try to run away, and Rufus and I could chase them down and punish them." Troy's eyes glittered at the thought.

Beaux spoke through the food filling his mouth. "I've been sitting out here, contemplating the viability of my business."

"You're making a killing."

"That's true, but it's never enough." He grinned. "You know how we make our money on individual sales of our digital products on the dark web? This time around, I'm taking a page from the huge online retailers. Through an intricate code and cloaking system that keeps identities secure, I'm going to start a subscription-based sales model. We'll rake in millions on a steady, monthly basis. Our biggest challenge will be to provide enough fresh content to keep our customers happy."

"We can order more kids. I think there's as big a market for teens as there is for children—you know, young bodies just beginning to change, but fully functional?"

"Hm. That might be exciting." Beaux let his mind frolic with the idea. If only it didn't take so long to acquire new merchandise and then train them.

He'd considered getting out of the drug and gun game

to loosen up more time, but he couldn't make himself let go of the cash. Even though he made significantly less with those income streams, it was still a healthy chunk, and for the most part, with the right people, it could run itself in the background. He could never have enough money. Human trafficking was a thirty-two-billion-dollar industry in the United States alone. And he wanted his cut. Beaux would gain world-wide reach with his new subscription plan. His goal was to control a massive share of that particular, untaxed market, and enjoy every minute doing it.

"Troy, I have a business proposition for you."

His bodyguard leaned forward, bracing his elbows on his knees. "I'm intrigued."

Beaux licked gooey cheese from his plump fingers. "What do you think of the title 'Damsel's Demise' for a feature film? I would cast you as the hero."

"Demise as in death?" Beaux nodded, and a spark gleamed in his bodyguard's eyes. "Would I get to wear a mask?"

CHAPTER 25

Dirk drove an hour and a half on gravel roads through the woods toward Sheriff Donnelly's last known coordinates. When he arrived, no one was there, but he studied the area and took pictures on his phone, anyway. A mile farther, he pulled to the shoulder and nudged Hank awake.

The kid pushed himself up in the seat and looked around, his hair stuck straight up, and his brow creased. "Where are we?"

"Learn to sleep like that in the Army?"

Hank yawned and answered with a sleepy grin.

"We've been to Molly's house. No one was there. And to the Sheriff's Department where I filed a missing person's report on her."

"Man," Hank stretched the best he could in the confined area of his seat, "I feel like we just left the office a few minutes ago."

"Glad you got some rest. You needed it. The sheriff was MIA again, so I had Manning track his cruiser. I followed the coordinates out here to the middle of Nowhere, Montana hoping to find out what he's up to. But there's no one out this way, and besides, he could be anywhere by now."

Hank brought up Google Maps on his phone and zoomed in. "There is literally nothing out here, except one house up the way another couple of miles. We could stop in and see if he's there or, if not, ask if anyone has seen a cop car driving around."

"I guess it's worth a try since we've come all this way." Dirk followed the map to the home. Tall logs stood perpendicular on either side of the drive. They supported a crossbeam from which hung an iron sign that said, "Wind Willow Ranch" with two W's intertwined beneath the name.

Dirk turned onto the road, and Hank snapped a photo. "I'll dig around and find out who owns this place and that brand."

The gravel road was almost a mile long and led to a luxurious log cabin home. Dirk stopped before a grand front entrance. "This house is incredible. Something tells me if anyone is home, they haven't seen the sheriff."

"Think this is a cattle ranch?" Hank stared at the opulent spread.

"I don't know. Since there's brand under the name on the gate, it probably was once, if it isn't still." Dirk got out of the car, and Hank followed him up a stone path.

Eight brightly colored cushions sat perched on pine rockers, welcoming them as they climbed the steps. The elaborate double-door entrance was hand-carved into a woodland nature scene, and stained-glass sidelights complimented the art. Dirk pressed the doorbell.

Rummaging sounded on the other side of the doors, and Dirk rested his hand on his waist above his holster. But no one came. Another noise echoed from inside. "Was that a kid crying?"

"Could be. Sounds far away, though. Maybe they can't hear the bell."

Dirk tried it again, ringing twice for good measure. The noise inside the house stopped. After waiting a few minutes longer with no answer, they left the porch and wandered around to the backyard. There was a walkout basement with a firepit and barbeque area, under a massive multilevel deck, but no people to be seen.

"Oh well, we should head back to Red Lodge and grab something for dinner. It'll be dark soon." Dirk and Hank returned to the car. "Hold on. I'm going to stick a business card in the window of the front door to let them know we stopped by."

"Good idea because we're probably on candid camera. If I owned a hootch like this, I'd have cameras all over the place."

The two men met at Dirk's Rubicon and drove off the property. Hank scrolled through his phone as they turned back toward Red Lodge. "Whoa. Stop. Can you pull over for a sec?"

Dirk stopped on the shoulder of the road. "What's up? I'd like to get back to town before dark."

"Nothing, but I have coverage here. Let me text Amy real quick, then you can drive again."

While he waited for the text conversation to end, the sun sank behind the mountains, leaving pink and blue streaks across the sky. Dirk noticed a car pull out of the drive behind them. It sped up and passed them by. Dirk pulled out to follow the brown sedan and matched the car's speed.

"Hold on. I'm not done yet." Hank tapped on his phone screen.

"It'll have to wait." Dirk flipped a switch, and red and blue lights flashed from the grill and side mirrors of his Jeep.

Hank hit send and tossed his phone in the console. "What's happening?"

"That car came out of the ranch property. I'm going to pull him over and see who he is."

"You know it's not illegal to ignore a knock at your door, right?"

Dirk shot Hank a sardonic glance. "I'm aware."

The car pulled to the side of the road and waited for Dirk and Hank to approach. Inside sat a man in his late thirties wearing a white tunic. He rolled down his window.

"Good evening," Dirk said as he approached the driver's side. Hank remained at the back right corner of the sedan.

"Good evening, officer. Was I speeding?" A delectable scent floated out from the open window.

Dirk's stomach responded greedily. "Probably, but that's not why I pulled you over tonight." He showed the man his badge and ID. "I'm Deputy US Marshal Sterling. I'd like to see your license and registration, please."

The man complied, staring at him nervously while Dirk read and checked the identification. "Where are you headed, Mr. Green?"

"Home."

"So, the house you just left isn't yours?"

The driver chuffed. "Hardly. I'd never be able to afford a place like that. My house could fit inside their garage. No, I just work there."

"What kind of work do you do?" Dirk peered around the car's interior while he questioned the driver.

"I'm a chef. I cook for the people who live there."

"Must be why your car smells so good."

Green glanced at the passenger's seat. "Left over Chateaubriand."

Dirk pointed to some beads hanging from the rearview mirror. A photo of the driver with a woman and a little girl swung from the end of the lanyard. "Is that your family?"

Green reached for the picture, and a smile brightened his face. "Yeah. That's my wife and our little girl, Tina."

"Let me show you a picture." Dirk found the image he wanted on his phone and held it up for the man to see. "Do you recognize this man?"

Green cocked his head and narrowed his eyes. "Maybe. Why do you want to know?"

"Is he your employer?"

"I'm not comfortable answering questions about someone else. Especially if it could cost me my job."

"So, yes?" Dirk waited.

"Is he in trouble?"

"Let's just say the man we're looking for is heavily involved with human trafficking and child molestation." Dirk pointedly shifted his gaze to the man's family. "If I were you, I wouldn't want anything to do with someone like that."

"Oh, my God. Are you serious?" Shock sucked the air from Green's lungs. "Yes. Yes, that's the man I work for. I didn't know. You have to believe I would never knowingly work for a man like that."

"Are there any children in that house?"

"I think so. I never saw them, but Johnny asked me to make a couple of trays of peanut butter and jelly sandwiches before I left. I normally only cook dinner, but today was lunch and dinner." He covered his mouth and looked like he might be sick. "Thank God I never took Tina over there."

"Is the man currently at the house?"

"No, I don't think so. He and his bodyguards left right after dinner. I don't have any idea where they went."

"Okay. You've been a big help. I suggest you go straight home and stay there. And if I were you, I'd call in sick tomorrow."

"Absolutely. Thank you for letting me know."

"Have a good night. Drive safe."

CHAPTER 26

When they got back in the Rubicon, Dirk said, "We aren't going home now. I'll go back to the spot where you had coverage so you can explain to your wife, and I'll call the chief and tell her we have found our fugitive." He didn't give Hank an option, but Amy wouldn't care. She'd accused him of staying away from home on purpose, just to avoid her. Which, as awkward as their relationship had become, her claim was not true.

At the side of the road, Dirk called Chief Grey while Hank texted: **Think we found the man we've been hunting. Can't come home until we confirm. Call u in the am.** He turned his phone off, not wanting to deal with her response.

"Grey isn't answering. I left a message that we were going to do some recon. You ready?"

"Always."

Dirk drove about a mile past the ranch entrance and

pulled into a stand of trees, effectively hiding his black Rubicon. He popped open the flip-up window in the back where he kept his tactical gear secured. Hank joined him there and they suited up, packing necessary weapons, instruments of observation, and basic survival items—water and energy bars.

They hiked back toward the ranch road, traveling through trees and underbrush to avoid detection. A mile in, Hank caught the glint of headlights. He gestured to Dirk who nodded that he'd seen them. Silence was the name of the game as they crept closer to the location of interest.

They made their way to the edge of the trees on the top of a ridge that towered over a mountain meadow and stream. Rippling water danced in the moonlight. He would sure love to live in a place like this, but it was not in his cards. Besides, Hank was content in his apartment in Billings. Or he would be, if Amy could be happy.

Hank pointed to some movement down below. Two large men, a muscular one who moved like he knew how to handle himself, and a strutting obese man walked from the deck toward the barn and disappeared inside.

Dirk flipped the lens cover off his binoculars and focused on the men below. "That's Crandall! The fat one. I'm sure of it."

Hank scrambled to peer through his own lenses, and adrenaline mule-kicked him in the chest. "Holy shit! You were right all along, Sterling!" He lowered his binos. "What do you think they're up to?"

"Probably the same crap he did in Louisiana. But this time, we're going to catch him red-handed and send him to prison. Go set up on the far end of the trees before the stream breaks the line. Settle in. We'll watch until we have a reason to move. I'll message the chief, again. If we end up going in, I don't want to be doing it alone."

CHAPTER 27

At 11:00 pm, two black Suburbans glided out of the barn. They drove around the paddock to the front porch of the log home where a man of medium height and weight wrestled a woman of a similar size down the steps. He shoved her toward the open back door of the first vehicle.

"Is that Molly?" Hank's voice came through Dirk's earpiece.

"I can't tell for sure with the black bag over her head. The woman's build is the same as Molly's, but I couldn't see her face or hair."

The man pushed the woman into the Suburban. He followed her in and closed the door behind them. A matching bookend partner joined the muscled man they'd seen earlier as they got out of the second SUV and opened the double back doors of the vehicle. They jogged into the house and several minutes later returned, shepherding a flock of small children. Dirk's stomach knotted into stone as he counted. Eleven.

The goliaths lifted the kids into the open back doors of the Suburban. Urgency spiked Dirk's nerves as he strained to see if any of them looked hurt or were crying. Instead, they looked like miniature zombies. Had they been drugged for easy transport?

Finally, the fat man, whom they now knew was Crandall, came out of the house. He stalked to the front seat of the SUV that held the woman. The two hulks Dirk assumed were bodyguards closed the doors on the kids, and each climbed into a driver's seat in one of the Suburbans and pulled away.

Dirk sprang to his feet, and without waiting, he called to Hank on the radio. "They're changing locations. We have to follow them, or we'll lose them!"

"We're over a mile from your Jeep."

"Then we run!" Dirk scrambled for his sat phone to call for back-up. He tripped on a rock and landed on his hands and knees, biting his lip in the process. The phone flew from his grasp, bouncing down the edge of the incline. "Damn it!" He spit out a stream of coppery tasting blood and wiped his mouth with the back of his hand.

He couldn't waste time retrieving the device besides, Hank had another one and they'd meet at the Jeep in ten minutes, tops.

Hank was faster and caught up to Dirk before they got to the car. Getting older sucked. "I dropped my phone. Call the Chief on yours and ask for eyes in the sky ASAP."

The partners threw their gear into the Rubicon and jumped inside. Spinning a gravel-spitting U-turn, Dirk tore down the road in pursuit. He saw no taillights in the darkness before them, but one thing in their favor was the single-lane dirt road went on for miles before there was anywhere to turn off. All Dirk and Hank had to do was catch up to them.

———

"Chief, this is Flannigan. We're in pursuit of two black Suburbans traveling northwest on back roads approximately seventy miles north of Red Lodge. We believe one of the men we're chasing is Beaux Crandall. He's accompanied by three other men, an unknown woman who appears to be a captive whom they forced into the front vehicle, and eleven children they're carrying in the second. When we first saw them, we were on foot, surveilling the house where we suspected Crandall was living. That's when everyone loaded up and left. Unfortunately, Sterling's car was over a mile away, so we got a late start in following them. We need eyes in the sky as soon as possible. We can't lose them."

"Eleven kids? My God. I'll call the FBI. I know they're looking for the kids in Edgar and will certainly want in on this. We'll use the FBI helicopter, and I'll track your phone for coordinates—so keep it on you. And stay out of sight until we get there to back you up." Keyboard strokes filled the pause. "ETA thirty minutes."

"Yes, ma'am."

Dirk pointed through the windshield. He'd spotted red taillights bouncing in the far distance and turned off his headlights. "There they are."

Hank relayed the information. "We've got them in sight. Tell the FBI to hurry."

"We're on the way. And Henry, you and Dirk stay vigilant!"

"Will do. I'll keep you posted." He ended the call and reached for his .300 Win Mag complete with a silencer resting in the back seat.

Keeping the taillights in view, Dirk followed far enough away not to be seen. It was difficult to navigate the road without headlights, and the crescent moon offered little help. They headed south on a straightaway and glimpsed the Suburbans before they made a sharp left turn off the path.

"Where are they going? There are no other roads out here." Hank squinted. He checked his phone, but nothing registered on Google Maps.

Dirk leaned forward in his seat, fully focused on the road before him. The red lights disappeared over a hill, and a bead of sweat popped out along Hank's hairline. "Hurry!"

Since the large SUVs were out of sight again, Dirk pressed on the accelerator but slowed as they approached the approximate spot where the Suburbans turned off. He clicked the headlights on just as they passed by a break in the barbed-wire fence.

"Did you see that?" Dirk jammed the Rubicon into reverse.

"Yeah. There's a gap in the barbed wire. But there's no road."

Dirk aimed the Jeep at the break. His headlights revealed a rarely traveled two-track path possibly worn in by a tractor or an ATV. Dirk turned onto the path and switched off his lights again. The rough road made for much slower going, but they could not afford to be seen.

Hank resisted getting out of the car, having an overwhelming rush of impatience at the thought that he could run quicker than they were traveling. "You gotta drive faster."

Dirk glared at him. "We can't risk them knowing we're here, kid. Breathe deep and hold onto your panties." He did not speed up.

Soon, they crested the hill where they last saw the Suburbans.

Hank's mouth fell open. "Oh my, God. This isn't on the map."

CHAPTER 28

The scene below glowed with powerful floodlights. A hangar the size that would fit a small jet stood before enough tarmac to maneuver said plane. Dirk reached for his binoculars. A runway extended into the dark, and though he couldn't clearly see the end of it, he estimated it was at least four-thousand feet. Long enough for a private jet to take off and land. A windsock blew toward the southeast, but there was no tower. This was an unmanned, and obviously unregistered, private landing strip.

Two men pushed open the sliding doors of the hangar, and the Suburbans stopped to the side of the entrance, remaining out of the jet's pathway. If he and Hank didn't get down there fast, they'd lose Crandall, for sure. Not to mention the woman and children whom they would likely never see again.

"We're going in." Dirk stepped on the accelerator, confident that with the floodlights blazing and the growl of the jet engines, no one could see or hear them coming.

"Shouldn't we wait for back-up? Chief Grey ordered us to stand down until the FBI chopper gets here. Besides, we're way outgunned."

"We have no time to lose, Hank. Those kids need our help now." Dirk's heart rate spooled as they raced toward the hangar, but his mind sharpened into stark focus.

Hank checked the magazine on his pistol and ran his hand over the spares on his vest. Dirk had done the same when they were on the ridge above the mansion. They were as armed as they were going to get. The opposition definitely had more firepower, and only a few more shooters. But Dirk and Hank had the element of surprise going for them, and with any luck, the FBI chopper would swoop in before it was all over.

As they sped toward the airstrip, a sleek Falcon taxied out of the hangar. The pilot shut the engines down. A few minutes later, the door opened, and the stairs folded down.

"It's likely that pilot is armed too, so don't forget about him," Dirk barked.

"And there are probably two pilots in that jet."

"So, our odds are sitting at twenty-five percent. No problem." Dirk pulled to a skidding stop at the edge of the lighted area. "We're on foot from here. You go right. Let's go!"

They gathered their weapons and separated. Each running along the perimeter of the light, getting as close as possible before they had to drop to the ground and low crawl the rest of the way in. Dirk took the chance and darted to a position behind the fuel tanks.

One of the Suburban drivers stepped out and approached the pilot. They spoke for several minutes, which gave Hank the opportunity to dash across the dark landing strip on the far side and take cover behind the building. Hank's voice came over the radio. "In position on the far side of the hangar."

"I see you. I've taken cover behind the fuel tanks."

"Copy that. Confirming, I see a second pilot inside the cockpit."

"Roger. We're going to have to hit these guys with shock and awe. Wait until all the players are out of the Suburbans. Then, I'll make a break for it. When I do, take out the two guards and if you can, disable the jet. As soon as I fire my first shot, blow these tanks with a couple of incendiary rounds."

"You're too close, Dirk. You won't be able to get far enough away from the explosion."

"I'll do it. Don't second-guess me. This is our best chance, and the timing is crucial. I won't shoot until I've covered enough distance."

Hank paused for a second longer than made Dirk comfortable. Finally, he growled, "Roger." Hank's military discipline overcame his doubt, and Dirk knew he'd follow orders even if he thought Dirk was cutting it too close.

The second driver exited his vehicle and conferred with his partner. Both men wore suit coats, which Dirk was certain covered a minimum of two firearms each, if not more. It was likely they also sported ankle holsters. He suspected they had even bigger firepower inside the Suburbans, and possibly some in the jet too. It was imperative he prevent them from reaching those weapons.

A third man—the one who'd manhandled the woman—was the next to step outside. He hitched up his belt and swaggered over to the guards and the pilot. Their lack of urgency gave Dirk confidence they had no idea someone was watching them.

"Come on, Crandall. Get out of the car," Dirk murmured to himself. His pulse rat-a-tatted as fast as the release of a fully automatic machine gun. In a vain hope that he'd see their back-up on its way, he glanced over his shoulder. He wiped sweat from his forehead before it dripped into his eyes and slowed his breathing.

Crandall's door swung open, and Dirk breathed in for four counts, held, and let it out for six. Shiny black wingtips touched down. In four… out four. *Come on, you son-of-a-bitch.*

The fat man hoisted himself out of the seat. "What's taking so long?" Crandall remained too close to the vehicle for Dirk to take a shot. In three…out three.

"Be ready," Dirk whispered in his mic.

"I'm on it, but you better run like hell… sir."

A smile curled one side of Dirk's mouth. "Will do."

Dirk crouched with his Glock 19 at the ready. The second Crandall closed his car door, Dirk sprang. He sprinted as fast as his legs would pump. "Drop your weapons! US Marshals!" he yelled.

The guard spun and fired at him. Dirk aimed at the man. As soon as he squeezed the trigger, all hell would break loose. *Prepare to meet the devil.* He fired, but the shot was wide, missing his target. Sprinting toward the plane, Dirk fired a second time and dove to the ground, rolling.

Both guards crouched into defensive positions. One dashed to put himself between Crandall and the shots.

Dirk's second shot had hit one of the guards as he was drawing his gun. It wasn't a fatal wound, but he'd be out of the mix at least for a little while.

A painful concussive sound slammed against Dirk's eardrums. He covered his ears, but it was too late. Agony seared inside his head, and he could not hear anything except for a high-pitched ring. A blast of heat lifted him from the ground, throwing him at least ten feet in the air. He landed hard on the tarmac, scraping his face and hands.

The explosion from the fuel tanks rocked the SUVs off their back wheels. The heat melted the rubber tires. Dirk swallowed, praying the children were safe. He had under-estimated the force of the blast.

He rolled again and sprang to his feet, aiming his gun at one of the jet's tires. Firing, he missed the wheel, but punctured the fuselage.

A burning sting singed his forehead, and his body went cold. A sober realization stole his breath. He'd missed instant death by a mere hair. Diving, he rolled for cover behind one of the jet's tires, but he'd given the guards too much time. They ducked behind their huge vehicles and were no doubt fortifying themselves with greater fire-power. Crandall was nowhere to be seen.

The pilot had disappeared too, but Dirk knew where he was as soon as the jet engines cranked up. He turned and fired three rounds into the fuel tank. With a compro-mised pressure hull and a leaking fuel tank, they wouldn't get far.

A barrage of bullets pelted the air around him in answer to his tactic. Those idiots were firing at their own escape plane.

Dirk emptied his magazine to keep the guards' heads down as he switched to the M4 Carbine strapped to his back. He took aim, but before he pressed the trigger, one of the guards' heads exploded—his rifle clattered to the ground, and he collapsed in a heap.

Hank! *Good work, kid.*

Crandall grabbed the dead guard's .308 and scurried behind the Suburban containing the children. He screamed, "Get the woman!" and dove into the SUV.

Dirk couldn't shoot at the vehicle without risking the lives of the hostages and now Crandall was inside too, no-doubt using them for cover. Coward!

The unidentified man stumbled out of the other SUV, holding Molly, the bag yanked half off her head, in front of him as a shield. "Drop your weapons! If you want to save this woman's life, you're gonna let us get on this plane and leave."

Dirk didn't hear the silenced spit of Hank's Win Mag, but the result was clear. The second guard dropped to the ground. His body convulsed obscenely for several seconds before it stilled.

Two down. Four to go, and twelve to rescue.

The jet pitched forward, stealing Dirk's cover. He ran alongside the Falcon until the nose swung toward him forcing him to jump out of the way. The nosewheel missed him, but the rain of fire did not. He took two shots. One in his left arm, the other in his vest.

He slammed onto the tarmac from the force, robbing his body of air. He fought to draw breath, but his lungs, screaming in pain, refused.

Hank responded by laying down cover fire to give Dirk the precious seconds he needed to move. He rolled to his feet, dizzy and still without enough oxygen. His lungs wailed, and his brain clawed for clarity.

"I will kill her!" the man yelled, firing his gun into the sky.

Good, let him waste rounds.

The pilots remained inside the jet, and though they had used the plane as a shield, they did not join the firefight. Laying his life on the bet that they were unarmed, or at least were unwilling to shoot, Dirk bolted toward the nearest Suburban. The one that held Crandall and the children.

He ran in a zig-zag line hopefully making himself harder to hit. Only one shot rang out before he dove to the ground in front of the huge grill. His arm shrieked with white-hot pain and he focused on pulling in more air.

"There are kids in here!" Crandall yelled. "I will kill them all if you don't throw down your weapons!" Crandall's voice roared from the dark depths of the SUV. Terrified cries from the children underlined his threat.

Dirk crept around the corner of the Suburban. He could not see inside the tinted windows. With the doors closed, there was no way to take Crandall out without risking the kids' lives.

Dirk had misjudged the pilots. The jet door opened, and the muzzle of a gun pointed out from the opening. Dirk leapt behind the SUV's front quarter panel before the pilot fired his weapon. Hank took him out with a shot to center-mass. The second pilot shoved his partner's body from the plane and retracted the stairs. The cabin door closed.

Molly screamed and fought her captor like a wild beast. Dirk pivoted back to the grill of the Suburban and took aim. As soon as he had a shot, he'd take it.

Giving everything she had, Molly bit, scratched, and kicked—throwing her body around. The man smashed his gun into the side of her skull. The skin at her temple split, and blood poured down her face. The blow stopped her efforts for a few seconds, but the man remained well concealed behind her. She roused and fought again with every ounce of herself until she caught the man in the nose with the back of her head.

He cried out in pain and reflexively shoved her away from him. Dirk recognized him in that second. Sheriff Donnelly! Shock coursed through him, igniting rage deep in his belly. The dirty sheriff fired his gun, and Molly's body went limp. She collapsed to the ground a split-second before Dirk's bullet ended Donnelly's miserable existence.

The jet engines surged to a roar. The Falcon turned for the runway. Hank fired several shots, but somehow the pilot managed to get the craft airborne. He wouldn't get far, but he might get away. Where the hell was their FBI back-up?

CHAPTER 29

"US Marshals," Dirk yelled, causing his bruised lungs to burn. He scrambled back behind the front corner of the Suburban in case Crandall drove it forward. "You're the only one left, Crandall. Throw your weapons out of the vehicle and stick both hands out the window."

"I don't think so, Deputy." The Suburban shifted as Crandall moved around inside. Dirk couldn't be sure where exactly he was in the big SUV.

"There's only one of two ways this is going to end for you. Either way, you lose. Give it up and live. Or don't—and die."

"You forget I'm surrounded by all these little kiddos, Deputy. There's no way you're gonna shoot into this car. So, here's how it's going to go down. I'm going to drive away from here, and you're going to let me."

Crandall was right, and he knew it. Dirk had to treat this as a hostage negotiation. "Say I'm willing to make a deal. You let the kids go, and we'll let you drive away."

"How stupid do you think I am?"

The problem was, Beaux Crandall was a lot of things, but stupid wasn't one of them. He was right. Dirk had no real options. He checked his watch wondering again where their back-up was. "What do you want to have happen? How do you see this thing turning out?"

"I want you to let me drive away."

"You've got to give me something in return. That's how a negotiation works. How about you release the kids and take me instead?"

"There you go again, thinking I'm a fool. I'll give you three of the kids as a measure of good faith. When I'm certain you aren't following me, I'll leave the Suburban with the rest of the children inside. When I'm free, I'll let you know where I left them. But if I find out you followed me, I will kill them all."

"I can't let you take the kids with you, Crandall."

"If you come any closer, I'll kill each one of them!"

"You won't get to them all before I put you down," Dirk bluffed. The children wailed, and his heart crumpled with guilt for scaring them more than they already were.

"Let me go, and I'll drop the kids off when I turn onto the road. I'll disappear, and we'll both win."

If the FBI back-up didn't get there in the next few minutes Dirk might not have any other choice. Could he bet on Crandall not wanting to manage eleven children on his own? There was no way he could disappear with all of them, but Dirk couldn't stomach Crandall's other more final option. The one he would most likely take.

Dirk's arm throbbed, and his fingers tingled. He flexed his hand, and a jolt of fire shot up to his shoulder. In the heat of the battle, he'd forgotten he'd been shot.

Reaching for the wound, he ran his fingers over his saturated sleeve. He'd lost a good amount of blood and needed to tie something around his arm to stop the flow.

"How do you see this going down, Crandall?" Dirk kept him talking to buy time.

Crandall's voice relaxed by a hair. "You lay your guns on the ground and step away from them. Your partner will have to do the same. Then, I'll start the engine and drive away. Easy."

Dirk spoke into his mic. "Hear that, Flannigan? You'll have to lay down your Glock and your M4."

"Affirmative. Waiting for your order."

They had only one chance, and Dirk had to take it. There were truly no other options. "Okay. I'm standing up and stepping away." He did as he'd said but kept his rifle in his working hand.

"Now put your weapons down. The rifle *and* your pistol." The SUV shifted again as Crandall climbed into the driver's seat. He held a little boy on his lap.

Dirk laid down his rifle, and holding one of his handguns in the air, he removed the magazine and set it, along with the pistol, down next to the rifle. He raised his good hand and continued to back away. His vision blurred, and he blinked for clarity. The painful throbbing in his arm demanded attention.

The car shifted again. "And your partner. I need to see him do the same thing."

"Okay, Hank. Your turn. On my count." Dirk gave the order.

"On it."

"First, lay down your service rifle." Dirk prayed all the

kids would make it out of this alive. They sure as hell wouldn't come out of this emotionally sound.

Hank knelt and set his M4 Carbine on the ground.

"Okay, now your Glock."

Hank repeated Dirk's process of removing the magazine and tossing both it and the gun to the pavement away from him.

"Okay, Crandall. I expect to find all these kids safe and sound a mile down the road, or so help me God, I'll hunt you to the ends of the earth and tear you to shreds."

"You're not really in a position to threaten me, Deputy."

Dirk kept Crandall's attention on him. "It's not an empty threat. How many kids do you have in there?" A shadowy glint crossed over the tinted glass.

In that second, Hank swung the Win Mag he wore strapped to his back, hidden from Crandall's sight, around and gripped it with both hands. He sprinted to the side of the Suburban undetected. Using the muzzle of the rifle to shatter the glass on the driver's side, he held the tip of the rifle to Crandall's temple.

Dirk reached for his secondary gun holstered on his low back and ran in a tight arc around the SUV's hood to the passenger's side. He yanked open the door, aimed his weapon at Crandall, and made a visual confirmation that no other men were inside. "Thank God, you read me loud and clear, kid."

The child on Crandall's lap was too frightened to cry and stared at Dirk with huge blue eyes. "You're safe now. Climb in the back with the other children. We're going to help you." The small boy nodded and scrambled away from Crandall.

Helicopter rotors echoed in the night sky as the FBI bird approached from above. While Dirk kept his gun leveled at Crandall, Hank yanked him out of the car and forced him to lie face down on the tarmac. With his knee in the fat man's back Hank cuffed Crandall's hands behind him. Dirk raced to the back of the Suburban and flung open the double doors. Eleven pairs of eyes stared out at him, and his knees buckled. He dropped to the ground.

"Dirk!" Hank called out, but he had to stay with Crandall until help came.

State Patrol cars led by a Carbon County sheriff's cruiser crested the hill with lights and sirens blazing. Dirk was vaguely aware of the helicopter landing, and Hank turning his captive over to the FBI.

Hank yelled, "Medic!" As he ran to Dirk's side. "Medic!"

Emory's worried face appeared over Hank's shoulder. Her green eyes were the last thing Dirk saw before everything went black.

CHAPTER 30

Emory had phoned Dave knowing he could fulfill her request faster than if she went through the official channels. She explained that Dirk and Hank had eyes on one of their Top Ten Most Wanted fugitives and that they had called for emergency back-up. "They need a helicopter spotter, right away."

"Who are they chasing?"

"Beaux Crandall out of Louisiana. He ditched his bail and was MIA for over a year, but he's resurfaced and set up shop here in Montana. Guns, drugs, and child pornography. He's holding a female and a bunch of kids hostage."

"Sounds like a job for the Hostage Rescue Team."

"I doubt we have time to get HRT. This thing is going down right now."

"What about the Marshall's bird?"

"It's all the way over in Missoula. Yours is closer and… I could catch a ride."

"Need to fly in and rescue Sterling again. Is that it?"

"Come on, Dave. This is serious."

"Yeah, I know. Let me see what I can do." He put her on hold for over five minutes. She was ready to hang up and call back when he finally returned. "Okay, text me the coordinates and be at the hangar in ten minutes."

"Thank you, Dave."

He clicked off with no response. She deserved his anger. That he could get past it and do the right thing proved what a good man he was. He didn't deserve her hot and cold inconsistency.

Emory grabbed her go bag and bolted to her car. If she was late, they'd leave without her.

She left her vehicle outside the FBI hangar and dashed inside. Dave waved her over, and she leapt aboard the Bell 407 behind him and buckled in. Before they even took off, Emory began contacting the various law enforcement agencies in the area who could provide support. She started with the Montana State Patrol and then called Deputy Manning. He promised to leave the station immediately.

Three separate agencies and departments converged on the coordinates Hank had sent her. The airstrip floodlights were easy to spot from the sky as were the stream of headlights racing toward the location on the ground. The pilot circled the hangar before setting down.

"It looks like Sterling is laying down his weapons." Dave pointed out the window. "Flannigan, too."

Emory couldn't believe what she was seeing. The next seconds had them thinking the deputy marshals had lost the battle when, in a flash, Dirk dove to the side and Hank swung his rifle from his back around his shoulder and smashed in the driver's window of one of the vehicles. Dirk pulled a handgun from his waistband and dashed toward the SUV.

"Put us down!" Dave commanded. Before the chopper's skids touched ground, the FBI Tactical Unit jumped out and raced toward the scene. As soon as they assessed that the situation was secure, they signaled to Dave and he and Emory ran toward the hangar. Dirk opened the back doors of the Suburban and a breath later he fell to his knees before collapsing completely on the ground.

Henry sprinted across the tarmac to Dirk's side. Had he been shot? Was there another shooter inside the Suburban? Terror clutched at Emory's heart, and she screamed, "Dirk!" She launched toward him with Dave right behind her. Patrol cars with their lights blaring were everywhere. The night erupted in confusion. Hank yelled for a medic. The only one around was from the tactical unit, and she raced to Henry with her Trauma Response Gear.

Emory gripped Henry's shoulders as she peered over him. Dirk's dark, fathomless eyes found hers seconds before they closed, and all the tension left his body.

"Dirk!" she cried. "What happened, Henry? Was he shot?"

Members of FBI SWAT lifted the children from the back of the SUV and passed them to a State Patrol Officer who had been an EMT earlier in his career. He assessed them one at a time.

Henry held Dirk's head, cradled on his knees. "Come on, Dirk. Come on, Buddy. Stay with me," he murmured, his gaze distant. Emory wondered if he were fighting battlefield ghosts even as he tried to save his partner.

"Someone tell me what is going on with my deputy!" she demanded.

"He has a gunshot wound in his upper left arm, and there is a plug in his body armor right over his heart. He's lost plenty of blood. He most likely lost consciousness due to a flood of adrenaline, low blood pressure, and the intense concussion he experienced against his chest wall. We must get him to a hospital immediately." The medic turned to a fellow agent. "Bring the stretcher right away!"

"Henry, I'll go with Dirk. You stay here. You're in charge of this crime scene. You can handle it. I believe in you."

Henry looked up at her as though he didn't recognize her and cold flushed through her veins. He was in no state to take command. But seconds later his eyes cleared. He helped ease Dirk onto the stretcher and then stood straight and tall before her. "Yes, ma'am. I've got this. But please, don't leave his side."

"I'll stand guard over Dirk, and I'm counting on you here."

Dave touched her elbow. "I'll stay with Hank. Don't worry about this mess. We'll handle it."

Emory's heart was wrung out. She was stupid to let a man like Dave slip away. But her squishy heart was none the less stubborn and was already inside the chopper with Dirk.

"It's okay, Emory. Good guys are used to coming in last. The soft laugh he delivered the words on held sorrow rather than humor. "I just hope Sterling appreciates how lucky he is. Go."

She reached up and kissed Dave's cheek. "I'm truly sorry. I wanted us to work. But—"

"But your heart belongs to that cocky son-of-a-bitch in the helicopter. I understand, but he damn well better treat you right."

"We aren't… he's… Dirk works for me. So, we don't have that kind of future. But it isn't fair of me to offer only half of my heart to you."

"If it were as much as half, I'd take it. You'll figure it all out, but for now, you better get on that bird, or it will take off without you."

She tried to smile as she bobbed her head. Pivoting, she dashed for the helicopter.

Emory sat in the back out of the way but close enough to hold Dirk's hand. Minutes after he was put on an IV and oxygen, his eyes blinked open and darted around in confusion. When his gaze rested on her, his body relaxed.

"Hey. You're going to be fine. We're on our way to the hospital now."

Memory of the recent scene must have hit him. His eyes hardened, and he tried to sit up, tearing the oxygen mask from his face. "There are children!"

The medic ordered, "Deputy, lie still and keep this mask on your face. Don't make me have to restrain you."

"It's okay. Don't worry. Henry and Dave are in charge of the scene. The children are all safe and are receiving care."

"Crandall?"

"In custody of the FBI." Emory squeezed his fingers. "It's over."

"I couldn't save Molly. I tried—" He searched her eyes. Then he grimaced—pain giving his skin a sallow hue—his body curled in agony, and he ground his teeth rather than cry out.

"What's happening, agent?" Emory gripped the medic's arm as fear engulfed her, leaving her overwhelmed with helplessness.

"Probably a muscle spasm in his chest. He could have broken ribs, even a bruised heart." She turned to the pilot. "Can we speed this rust bucket up?"

Emory fell to her knees to be closer to Dirk. "It's going to be okay. We're almost there. Hold on."

"I'm fine," Dirk growled.

"Right." She prayed he would be.

———

Christ, that hurt. Was he having a heart attack? Dirk resisted with everything he had not to scream out in pain. Emory looked horrified, and he didn't want to scare her any further. He coughed and a red-hot jolt seared his chest, paralyzing his heart again. He fought to draw in air.

"Keep breathing, Deputy. You need the oxygen to stay ahead of the pain."

"His name is Dirk." Emory fussed with the tubes attached to him and unshed tears wobbled at the corners of her eyes.

"I'll be okay, Em."

"You better be." She pasted a brave smile on her face and brought his palm to her cheek.

The FBI medic caring for him squeezed Emory's hand reassuringly. "I'm going to give him something for the pain now. He'll sleep from here on." The agent turned her gaze to Dirk. "Deputy, I'm giving you something that will make you sleep. You won't feel any more pain. We'll be at the hospital in ten minutes. Okay?"

"Roger that." He watched the needle enter the IV tube, then shifted his gaze. He focused on Emory's emerald eyes and her beautiful face until his eyelids grew heavy and slammed shut.

CHAPTER 31

irk's awareness slogged through his petroleum jelly covered consciousness. Had he fallen asleep at a party? Where the hell was he? He blinked open his eyes. The bright light caused his head to ache. Hank was at his feet laughing at something Ceylon just said. *Ceylon?*

He tried to sit up, but someone had placed a load of bricks on his chest. An alarm sounded somewhere, and everyone in the room turned to stare at him. What had he done?

Emory was there. She moved to his side. "Good morning." She touched his cheek. Wait, that couldn't be right. No way would she touch him like that in front of all these people—it had to be a dream. He tried to speak, but something was in the way. In his mouth. In his throat. He reached to shove it away.

"No, you don't!" A woman wearing Piglet pajamas rushed toward him and pushed his arm to the side. "I know it's uncomfortable, and I'll remove it. But you have to let me do the work, okay?"

His mind gradually cleared, and he remembered the scene at the private airstrip. He had vague images of being with Emory inside a helicopter. His body hurt, and his head was fuzzy. He was in the hospital. The situation was making much more sense—and the woman wore scrubs, not pjs. He nodded that he'd allow her to do her job.

The nurse switched off the alarm and undid the tape stuck to his face. "Okay, relax and we'll go on three. One…" Without waiting for the second count, she pulled the intubation tube out smoothly before he had a chance to resist. "There you go." She smiled at him. "It's best not to talk too much right away. You can have a few ice chips, but nothing else until the doctor sees you. Got it?"

"We'll keep an eye on him," Hank said. "He's not good at following the rules."

Dirk glared at him and told his lips not to grin. They didn't listen. One side of his rebellious mouth curled up. Must be the drugs.

"Okay, then. I'll let the doctor know you're awake." She turned to the crowd. "He won't approve of having so many people in the patient's room. Maybe you could take shifts? There's a nice waiting area just down the hall."

Hank herded Amy, Laurie, Caleb, and Ceylon into a group and guided them toward the door. "Come on every-one, you heard the nurse." Over their heads, he raised his chin at Dirk. "We'll be down the way." He pulled the door closed behind them, leaving him alone with Emory.

Before he could say anything to her, the doctor entered the room. He nodded at Emory and then addressed Dirk.

"We had a successful surgery last night to repair your left arm, and you have a good prognosis. You lost a fair amount of blood, but you'll quickly replace that with a healthy diet. Good protein, lots of water, and green leafy vegetables.

"There are five stitches on your forehead from what I believe was a bullet that came close enough to burn and split your skin. You, sir, are an extremely fortunate man. Any closer, and we wouldn't be having this conversation. Amazingly, you did not sustain a concussion, but it's likely you will still get some bad headaches over the next few days.

"My biggest concern was the round you took to the chest of your Kevlar vest. But, once again, you were lucky. You have significant bruising on your sternum, and you have a fractured rib. But God clearly knew what he was doing when he built the human ribcage to protect our organs. Your heart is fine. You are going to be quite sore, but there's not much we can do to help with that other than prescribe pain meds. You need rest. The question is, will you take it?"

"Sure," Dirk answered and saw Emory roll her eyes.

"You'll feel better faster, if you do." The doctor signed a couple of papers and left them on the table next to Dirk's bed. "I'd like you to remain here today and overnight for observation, but I don't see any reason you can't get out of here tomorrow morning."

"Thanks, Doc," Dirk rasped.

The doctor nodded at Dirk and then at Emory and left the room. Emory found a paper cup and filled it with ice bits left by the nurse. She spooned some out, offering it to him. The last thing he wanted was to be fed like a baby and he raised a single sardonic brow to communicate his thoughts.

"Everyone needs a little help once in a while, Dirk. Get over it." Her face brightened with a soft smile. "You scared me last night, you know."

"Nothing to worry about. You heard the doctor. I'm fine. Just a little lack of blood." His throat burned when he spoke.

Emory gave him another spoonful of ice. "Right. And surgery to repair your arm along with stitches on your forehead, a fractured rib and bruised sternum. It was too close of a call."

Dirk reached up and felt the bandage on his head. "I'd forgotten about this until he said something."

"Seriously?"

He smirked. "What happened with Crandall?"

"The FBI took him into custody. He's in a federal detention center waiting for his arraignment. Obviously, he won't get bail this time."

"And the kids?"

"They have each received medical care and Social Services returned them to their families, but they will need years of therapy to overcome what Crandall put them through."

"Sheriff Donnelly killed Molly." His statement caused his heart to ache, joining with the groan of pain in his bones. "That poor woman. Her only crime was trusting a snake."

Emory nodded and ran her fingers down the length of his good arm. "I'm just thankful you and Henry made it out of there alive. It wasn't the best plan to take all of those guys on by yourselves. I told Henry to wait for back-up. Why did you override my order?"

"We wanted back-up, but if we waited, Crandall would have flown those kids off to God knows where, to live a life of abuse and slavery. Their families would never have seen them again." Dirk fought to keep his eyes open even as fatigue weighed his lids down. "Whatever happened with the jet? Could the FBI track it?"

"The pilot didn't make it very far. He ran out of fuel and crashed into a mountain outside of Bozeman."

Satisfied with that, Dirk drifted. Before he dipped into deep sleep, Emory's lips brushed his cheek. His eyes flew open, and he grabbed her forearm before she could leave. Startled, she gasped.

"So—where's Dave?"

"Dave? Why, did you expect him to be here?"

"I expected him to be with you. What's going on, Emory?"

A beautiful shell-pink blush colored her cheeks, and she dropped her gaze to the floor. "Dave and I... we've decided not to see each other anymore."

"Why?" Suddenly alert, Dirk studied every nuance of her expression.

"I couldn't give him what he wanted—what he deserves."

"And what is that?" Dirk knew he was being an ass, but he had to know. This push-me-pull-you thing between Emory and him had to stop. It was driving him crazy. He found himself hating a perfectly decent guy simply because he had the license to touch Emory—to kiss her, to—Dirk's muscles shuddered at the thought of Emory and Dave together.

"Dave deserves a woman who can give him her all, especially all of her heart. I can't offer that. I'm not sure I can offer my all to anyone." She pulled her arm from his grasp.

"Why not?" She was slipping away again, and he was helpless to stop her, held in the bed with wires, tubes, and exhaustion.

"Because, I pour myself into my career. It's how I choose to live my life."

"Is that the only reason?"

"No. You know it isn't, Dirk. Why are you making me say what we both already know?"

"Because, once everything is out in the open, then we can figure it out."

She lifted her gaze to his then. Her moist irises glinted like fractured shards of bottle-green glass. "I don't see how." She reached down and squeezed his hand before she turned and left the room.

CHAPTER 32

Hank agreed to take Amy home now that they knew for sure Dirk was going to be okay. "Will you drive? I'm exhausted."

"We need to talk."

Those words always caused Hank's defenses to fly up. "Can it wait until after I have a nap?"

Amy's shoulders drooped, and she frowned but nodded her head in the affirmative. "I guess. How about we go out for lunch after you sleep?"

Something was up, and Hank went from sleepy to full alert. "Why don't you just spit it out now? I know you're upset about the incident last night. I'm sure seeing Dirk in the hospital was unnerving. Is that it?" He clicked the key fob and unlocked the car.

Amy opened the driver's door and climbed in, but Hank hesitated. He didn't have the energy to fight, and especially not when they were confined in Amy's Prius. Taking a deep breath, he braced himself for an onslaught. He got in the car and reclined his seat.

Amy pulled out of the parking garage. "Yes, you're right about my being upset about what happened last night. That could have been you in the hospital. I think seeing Dirk there and knowing that Laurie's husband was killed in the line of duty has given me a terrifying perspective."

"The odds of getting seriously hurt on the job are really low. What happened last night was an unusual situation. Normally, we wouldn't go into a situation like that without a full Special Operations Group or SWAT back-up. We found the airport by coincidence and didn't have time to wait for the team. That almost never happens. Besides, Dirk got hurt because he took calculated risks. He didn't allow me to be in the same danger. I was behind cover the entire time."

"You are full of hero worship for Dirk Sterling, but I think he's reckless."

Hank swallowed his ire. She wasn't there and didn't understand. "Maybe, but because of what he did last night, Social Services returned every one of those kids to their families. Dirk believed risking his life was worth that outcome."

Amy sighed. "I know. And I'm sure their parents are beyond grateful to him. To both of you. It's just scary being the one waiting at home to hear if you're dead or alive."

"I get that, but you knew what my job was going in. It wasn't any different in the Army."

"Maybe, but it didn't seem that way to me." Amy merged onto the highway.

"Is that because you had friends and activities to keep you from worrying?"

Amy defensively crossed her arms over her chest,

Hank held up an open hand. "Hear me out and don't get pissed. This is a legitimate question. Do you think you're reacting to the hormones you're on?"

She rolled her lips between her teeth and said nothing for several miles. "That might be some of it. But there are other things to talk about. Let's finish this discussion after we both have some rest?"

Maybe he would sleep all day and wake up after Amy went to bed for the night. Whatever she planned to say to him, it was likely going to change his life forever. He wasn't ready to call it quits, but if she had already given up on them, there was nothing he could do about it. As his mind drifted, he wondered if she'd be willing to try counseling. He could quit his job, but then he'd be miserable. That couldn't be the only answer, could it?

When they arrived at their apartment, Amy pulled up to the sidewalk. "We're home. Why don't you go on inside and finish your nap. I'm going to do a little shopping before our lunch date. I'll be back in a couple of hours."

Hank blinked sleep from his eyes and rolled out of the car. He was grateful not to have to hold a conversation as he fumbled through the door and onto the bed. Sleep took over, and he sunk so deep not even his dreams could find him.

When he finally woke, it was almost four-thirty, and the apartment was silent. He bolted upright. Bright lights glittered through his vision, and his heart pounded with an alarm-level pulse making him dizzy. "Amy?"

He padded into the bathroom and splashed cold water on his face to chase away the residue of deep sleep, and then rushed out to the living room. His wife was on the couch, knitting. *Knitting?*

"You're here." Relief filled his voice.

"Where else would I be?"

"I…" Deciding not to address her question, he changed the subject. "I didn't know you knitted."

"I haven't done it in years. I'd forgotten how soothing it is."

"Hmm."

"You slept all afternoon. Let's go to dinner, instead."

"Let me hop in the shower. I'll be ready in ten."

They didn't talk on the way to the restaurant. A new peace had settled on his wife's features, and that caused him to be more nervous than her anger ever did. Had she come to a place where she no longer cared? Had she made a decision about them that, once made, took her ire away? He knew that anger—or even hate—were not the opposite of love. Indifference was. Is that how Amy was feeling? Indifferent toward him? Toward their marriage?

Hank braced himself for the worst as he held the restaurant door open for her and pulled out her chair. They both behaved with extreme manners and politeness.

After Hank ordered a bottle of wine, Amy rested her hand on top of his. "I have something I need to tell you."

Hank closed his eyes and swallowed. He then met her direct gaze with one of his own. "Okay."

Her pupils dilated, and her mouth softened. "I'm pregnant. You're going to be a dad."

Hank stared at her. He blinked his lashes. The words she spoke were dissonant from what his mind and body were prepared to hear. He scrunched his brows together. "What?"

"Aren't you happy?" Worry lined her expression.

"What?" He needed to get a grip on his thoughts. Did she just say they were having a baby?

Amy's eyes glistened with gathering tears. "You're upset. You never wanted this, did you?"

"No! Amy, I'm not upset." He grasped her hand. "I'm just stunned. I thought… Never mind what I thought. Really? You're pregnant? Are you sure? Have you gone to the doctor?"

She laughed a light tinkling sound, and her cheeks pinkened. "Yes, I'm sure. I took two at-home tests and then confirmed it with the doctor. We're having a baby!"

Hank sprang to his feet and rounded the table. He pulled her up from her seat into his arms. "That's amazing news. I wasn't sure if we could… but we did! Congratulations, sweetheart!"

"Are you happy?" Her voice was small, and his heart ached with regret for the uncertainty he'd caused.

"I'm elated!" Hank raised his hand to get the waiter's attention. "Change the wine order to champagne. We are celebrating."

Amy laughed. "I can't drink, silly. Not now that I'm carrying precious cargo."

"Oh—right. Sorry," he called out to the server's back. "Cancel the bubbly. We'll have sparkling water instead." Relief swam through Hank's blood, making him feel a little tipsy. He'd been sure they were on the brink of divorce. Now maybe he and Amy could get their marriage back on track. They had nine months to fix things before their difficulties could affect their little human.

He helped Amy back into her chair, being overly cautious with her.

She laughed at him. "I have not suddenly turned into a China doll."

"I want to be careful."

"I'll be fine, but maybe you'll manage to be home more often now."

Well, that didn't take long. Hank's chest deflated several inches, but he chose to ignore the comment. Habits took time to change. But he was determined to make those changes. Things would definitely get better between them. They had to.

CHAPTER 33

Dirk was finishing his breakfast of scrambled eggs, bacon, and fruit when Hank arrived at the hospital the next morning.

"What? Wouldn't they make you smiley-faced pancakes? Those bastards!" Hank teased.

"Ha ha. You're never going to let that go, are you?"

"Not on your life." Hank pulled the visitor's chair to the side of Dirk's bed. "When will the doctor release you?"

"He already did. Now I'm waiting on the paperwork. Shouldn't take too long."

"Great. I bet you'd like to get home."

"Absolutely. No one can rest in a hospital."

"But will you rest at home?"

Dirk quirked his mouth sideways. "Of course, I will."

"Right. When do you start PT?"

"As soon as they take out the stitches."

"Good, because I don't want to get stuck doing all your work for months while you relax in the lap of leisure."

"Whatever. You'll do it and you'll like it." Dirk popped the last chunk of watermelon into his mouth.

"I stopped by your house and got you the button-up shirt you asked for. Do you need help getting dressed?"

"No. I'm not an invalid."

Humor glinted a challenge in Hank's eyes as he handed Dirk his shirt and returned to the chair, clasping his hands behind his head. He stretched out his long legs and crossed them at the ankles. Dirk ignored him and tugged on his jeans. The effort caused his head to swim, and he waited until he regained his equilibrium and some energy before he tried the shirt. His right arm was easy but slinging the fabric over his bandaged shoulder proved impossible.

Hank, not moving, watched from his chair, laughing silently at Dirk's efforts. Dirk hated asking for help, but if he was ever going to get out of there, he had to give in. "Alright, smart ass. Will you *please* help me with my shirt?"

"I'd be more than happy to." Hank took hold of the sleeve. Dirk's arm was in a sling, so Hank buttoned the shirt only halfway up leaving room for his hand and the brace. "I brought you your flip-flops too, since we're just going from here to your house."

"Good thinking, kid. Thanks."

After the nurse returned with the release paperwork, a prescription for pain meds, and gave an admonishment to both men about diet and rest, she pushed Dirk in the obligatory wheelchair to the front door of the hospital. Hank ran ahead to get his truck and met them at the entrance.

Hank held out both of his hands, spotting Dirk's movements as he climbed into the truck. "My legs work just fine, Nurse Flannigan."

"Get in and let me buckle your belt."

This kind of help made Dirk feel like a little kid and drove him mad. It was a short drive, but it was draining. More than anything, Dirk wanted to lie down and sleep. Hank helped him inside, and set him up on the couch, so he could watch TV if he wanted to.

"Are you hungry? I got some stuff from the store to make your lunch. How does a French dip sound? You need the iron for making more blood."

"You cook?"

"A little." Hank set a grocery bag on the kitchen counter and pulled out a bottle of wine, a package of beef, and some French baguettes. He held up the cabernet. "This is for a marinade. Not for you. No drinking while on narcotics."

Dirk was impressed. He'd have been happy with a turkey and cheese, but if the kid was going to cook, he wouldn't refuse. "I'm at your mercy, Nurse Flannigan."

"And don't forget it. Remember the movie *Misery*?"

Dirk rolled his eyes dramatically. He searched for a witty comeback, but the trip home had worn him out. He rested his head against a pillow and drifted off.

He woke again to Hank whistling in the kitchen as he set dishes on a tray. "Here we are," he said grinning as he carried a delicious-looking lunch to the coffee table.

The savory scent of beef, toasted bun, au jus, and horseradish made Dirk's mouth water and his stomach roar with hunger. He pushed himself up to receive the lunch. "This looks amazing, kid. Thanks."

Dirk dipped the corner of his beef sandwich into the au

jus and took a bite. A drip of the juice ran down his chin as he savored the flavorful sandwich. "This is fantastic. Where did you learn how to cook?"

"Here and there. It's something I enjoy." Hank sat on the coffee table across from Dirk, wearing a huge clown smile.

"What is going on with you? You've been grinning like a lunatic all morning."

Hank's smile broadened. "I have some news."

"What news?"

"You're gonna be an uncle."

Dirk scrunched his brows together. "What are you talking about? I don't have any siblings." Hank laughed, and it dawned on Dirk what his partner was trying to say to him. "Wait. Are you?"

Hank jumped to his feet and rounded the table. Excitement bounced off him like electric ping-pong balls. "Amy is pregnant!"

"That's great, kid!" Dirk was thrilled for them, but he was also concerned. "But is this what you want? I mean, I know you two have been going through a rough patch."

"I'm so excited, I can hardly sit still. I can't wait to have a little guy running around. Our problems had to do with going through the process of getting pregnant. Not with wanting kids."

Dirk's mouth stretched into a wide smile. His facial muscles were unaccustomed to such a large expression, but damn it, he was happy for the kid. "Congratulations! You're going to be a great dad."

"Thanks. I don't know about that, but I'll try." Hank performed a little happy dance with a disco spin at the end.

"Promise to never show the kid your dance moves."

Dirk chuckled. He thought back to the day Hannah told him she was pregnant. They'd only been kids themselves, and he had had no way to provide for a family, but he'd never been happier. Right after she gave him the news, he quit the rodeo, asked her to marry him, and joined the Marine Corps. That was as far as he allowed his memories to go.

Hank danced some more to music only he could hear, and then he grew serious. "I go between being over-the-moon excited, and terrified. I don't think I'm qualified to raise a little human."

"You'll do great, and when you screw it up, Amy will be there to fix it." Dirk winked at his friend. *Friend.* Yep. Hank had proven himself as a Deputy Marshal, as a partner, and also as a friend. Warmth filled Dirk's chest, temporarily erasing the ache in his ribs and sternum. Smiling, he drifted off to sleep.

CHAPTER 34

Emory tried to stay away, but by four in the afternoon, she'd convinced herself that Dirk would not eat well if left to his own devices, and that he was probably drinking beer instead of water. She stopped by the market after work to pick up supplies for a steak dinner and a few other necessities she knew he could use and drove to his home on the outskirts of Billings.

She'd never been to his house in town before, and it surprised her to see that it was an old farmhouse nestled in a stand of trees on a ten-acre lot. She pulled to a stop at the base of the steps of a recently painted, wide front porch. Red plaid cushions softened the seats of two wooden rockers and the bench of a porch swing—a bright splash of color against the white siding and glossy black shutters.

Emory knocked on the front door but let herself in, not wanting Dirk to get up to answer. "Dirk, it's me, Emory. I just brought some food by for dinner." She stepped inside and found herself face to chest with the man. "What are you doing up?" She tore her eyes away from the bare bruised skin under his open shirt. "Aren't you supposed to be resting?"

He took the grocery bag from her with his working arm. "I heard someone drive up. Plus, I've been resting all day. What'd you bring?" He set his bag on the counter and removed the contents one-handed.

"Everything for a steak and potato dinner, spinach salad, and corn on the cob. Brownies for dessert—if you're good."

"Oh—I'm good." He grinned and lifted the package of meat out of the bag. "There are two steaks in here. *Shirley* you'll be staying for dinner?"

Emory laughed at the play on words he loved to tease her with. "Are you ever going to stop reminding me of that night? You don't expect me to believe you've never used a fake name."

"Never." He set the corn on the cutting board. His phone buzzed from a table in the living room. "Would you mind grabbing that for me?"

"Sure." Emory hurried to catch the call. It was Henry. Without thinking, she answered it. "Hi, Henry. Hold on, I have to bring the phone to Dirk."

Dirk held the device to his ear. "Hey, kid. What's up?" As Dirk listened, the left side of his mouth curled into a mischievous grin. His eyes darted over to her. "Nah, I'm pretty sure nursing is part of her job description." He paused to listen. "Thanks, but the chief brought dinner, so I'm good for tonight. I appreciate it, though." He ended the call, and humor remained in his expression.

"I hope you are staying. Corn is a two-handed job, plus I'll need someone to cut my steak."

"Suddenly you're so needy." Emory shooed him from the kitchen. "I planned on cooking your dinner." She drew in a huge breath and held it until she gathered her courage. "And I had hoped you'd ask me to stay." Her eyes searched his, and an electric jolt coursed through her entire body, zinging out her toes.

———

The look in her eyes made his pulse jump. The increase stung like a mother, but he did his best not to let it show.

"What's wrong?" She dropped the corn cob and rushed to him, placing her hand on his forehead. She checked the sling on his arm and then rested her fingertips on his chest. "Is your heart okay?"

How the hell was he supposed to answer that? He knew she meant his physical heart, but that wasn't his problem. *Christ.* She was too close. Her touch inflamed his pulse further, and he swayed on his feet.

"You need to sit down, right now." Emory ushered him to the couch, and honestly, he was grateful to lie back against the pillow. "Don't get up again. I'm going to bring you some juice and then we'll have dinner here in the living room when it's ready."

Dirk closed his eyes and listened to her work in his kitchen. The domestic sounds comforted him even as he ordered himself not to go there. He drifted. Soon Emory sat his dinner plate on the coffee table. "Can you sit up to eat?" She felt his head for fever.

"Yes. And quit fussing over me." His tone was curt, but he needed to keep Emory at arm's length.

"Good." She ignored his surliness and helped him get situated.

Emory had cut all the food on his plate into bite-size chunks, and her care made him remorseful. "Sorry. I didn't mean to snap at you. Thanks for doing all this."

"You're welcome."

They ate side-by-side on the couch in a comfortable silence for a while, enjoying the view of the hayfields behind his house with the mountains in the distance on the horizon.

Dirk took his last bite of meat and stole a sip of Emory's wine. "Ceylon is coming down here to stay for a few days. I think she wants to practice her doctoring on me." He took a bite of potato. "Do you think I should be afraid?" He gave half a grin and glanced up for her answer. Was there disappointment in her eyes? Or was that just his overactive dream world, again?

"That's very kind of her." Emory moved her wineglass out of his reach to the other side of her plate. "No alcohol for you until you're off your pain meds."

"It was just a sip."

"Still. How long will Ceylon be here?"

"She can only stay a couple of days before she has to fly back to New York."

"What will you do then?"

"Come back to work."

"Dirk..." Her genuine expression of concern rocked him. Before he thought better of it, he reached for her, sliding his hand across her cheek. He ran his fingers into her hair and gripped the back of her head, pulling her toward him. He stopped a breath away from kissing her and stared into her eyes.

She responded by placing her hands on both sides of his face and pressing her lips against his. Frustrated that he only had one good hand, he leaned into her, tasting her, soaking her in. His chest blazed with pain, but he ignored it. Their kiss grew more heated, and his head swam with the sensations.

Emory backed away. The sudden loss of her heat, of her softness, was jarring. "What's wrong?"

"We… you…" she was out of breath, "you're hurt."

"I don't care."

"Dirk. If we do this, everything will change."

"Good."

"Maybe. But what if it *isn't* good? What if we can't make it work? That could ruin the lives we've both worked so hard to build."

As his blood cooled, he heard the wisdom in her words. If he let her in, she could crush him. He had built a wall around his heart so thick that no one could get in. His intention was for that kind of destruction to never happen to him again. Was he really prepared to open the fortified gate?

"You don't think we could behave like adults?" he asked her and himself.

"I think what we want is very risky."

He nodded. Riskier than she knew. If one day she decided she no longer wanted him, she'd move on. He wouldn't stop her or make a scene. Her career was safe with him. But he'd never survive the kind of heartbreak he'd gone through with his ex-wife a second time. He wasn't a man who could love halfway. Not getting involved at all was the safest choice.

"I know, you're right." The ache in his heart this time had nothing to do with his bruises.

She turned her face away and stared out at the view. "Okay." Her voice was barely more than a whisper. "I should go."

When she rose, a surge of emotions overcame his better judgment. He clasped her arm, pulling her down hard against him. A groan escaped his throat, and worry filled her eyes. "I'm good. Or I will be when you kiss me." He tugged her onto his lap, and she released a soft laugh. It was a beautiful musical sound that brightened the threatening darkness. She brushed her fingers over his face, tracing his mouth before bending to kiss him. He held her fast, holding her body tight to his.

This decision would likely be the end for him, but he simply couldn't refuse his longing. No matter what, his life was about to change forever.

CHAPTER 35

Emory ended up spending two nights with Dirk at his house. At least she'd found a way to keep Dirk in bed, if not exactly resting. It had been difficult to face her other deputies in the office. She felt like they could see right through her—that they knew exactly where she'd been sleeping. Her body had shivered with memories as she made her way to Dirk's kitchen the last morning. Henry had surprised her by showing up early with Ceylon for her visit.

He took everything in when he came inside Dirk's house that day, but he said nothing. He acted like it was the most normal thing in the world to see Emory at Dirk's place wearing one of his shirts and making coffee.

"Morning, Chief."

"Hi, Henry. Ceylon, good to see you. The coffee will be ready in just a few minutes. If you'll excuse me, I'll be right back."

Dirk walked out of his bedroom shrugging into a shirt. His hair was adorably mussed, and his morning scruff gave him a rakish look Emory found not only incredibly sexy but fitting. She made a conscious effort not to stare at him. Dirk too acted like everything was perfectly normal. *Men. How did they do that?*

"Hey kid, you're early. I thought you said late morning."

"Sorry about that." Henry's grin announced he was anything but sorry. "Traffic was light."

"There is no traffic between my cabin and here. Ever."

"Guess I should have figured that."

Dirk showed Ceylon to the guest bedroom, and Emory dashed into his room to get dressed. When she returned to the living room, Ceylon had settled in her bedroom and had started fussing over Dirk, taking his pulse and telling him to lie down while she made him tea. Did he even drink tea? Dirk was a good sport, though Emory knew it cost him. He hated the extra attention, and Emory hated that she wouldn't see him again until Ceylon went back to the Big Apple.

"Miss Emory, Hank, can I pour either of you a cup of tea?" Ceylon already seemed at home in Dirk's kitchen.

"No thanks, I'm a coffee drinker." Henry pulled two mugs out of the cupboard. "Chief?" He held one of them up, and she nodded gratefully. She breathed in the steamy richness from her mug, hoping it would fortify her nerves.

Dirk politely accepted the tea his new nurse offered him and winked at Emory over the brim of his cup.

Emory set a frying pan on the gas stove top. "I was just about to make Dirk some breakfast. Are you two hungry?"

Ceylon rushed in. "Oh, no. I'm happy to take over the caregiver job now that I'm here. I'll cook and do whatever

Dirk needs until he's back on his feet." She busied herself with making him a meal.

Emory dared a glance at Henry, whom she realized was dancing on the razor's edge of bursting into a full-blown laughing fit. "What is so funny?" she whispered.

Henry bit his lips together, and his eyes sparkled with humor. He murmured, "Just that Dirk gets to enjoy Ceylon fawning over him for two full days. I can only imagine how he's going to *love* that. He'll be begging to come back to work by the time she leaves."

"Henry, about me being here—"

He grew serious. "Ma'am, what happens between you and Dirk is none of my business. But I'll say one thing, and then I won't say anymore. I'm really happy for you both, and I'm honestly surprised it didn't happen before now."

Emory was stunned. "Really? Why?"

"You two have been dancing around each other ever since you came to Billings. Teresa and I have been placing bets."

"You have?" Emory's eyes widened, and her face flamed with heat.

Henry chuckled. "No, not literally. Let's just say it's obvious you two should be together. Now, I've got to go. I have a wife of my own who needs me." He gulped down the rest of his coffee and waved to Dirk and Ceylon as he went to the door.

"I'm right behind you. Lots to do before work tomorrow." Emory gathered her things and set them in the entry hall before saying her goodbyes. "Ceylon, before I go, tell me how your time up at the cabin was."

"It was a much-needed respite for meditation and reflection. I'm so thankful Dirk invited me to stay there."

"And are you ready for university next week?"

"Yes. For the first time in my life, I can see a clear path toward my dreams. I've wanted to be a doctor since I was a little girl, but people laughed at me or thought I was cute to have such an imagination. Here, in America, people like you, Dirk, and my sponsor believe in me. It makes me believe too. Thank you." Ceylon wrapped her arms around Emory's shoulders and held tight.

"I'm so happy for you, Ceylon. If you two need anything over the next few days, Dirk has my number, and I'd be happy to bring over whatever you might think of."

Dirk reached out his hand toward her, and Emory placed hers in his. "You don't have to go."

She squeezed his fingers. "Yes, I do. I have to get back to work, and you have company. Call me later."

"I wish you'd stay."

Emory bent down and left a lingering kiss on his cheek. "I'll see you soon."

CHAPTER 36

As usual, Emory was the first one at work on Monday morning. She and Dirk had talked about how things would be at the office; what the *new normal* might look like. Still, she was nervous.

Ceylon's flight to New York was at ten. Dirk would arrive at the office after he dropped her at the airport. Emory's nerves jittered. She prayed she and Dirk could make their relationship work at the office—that she wouldn't find him too distracting. Emory chuckled at her thoughts. Hell, Dirk had been distracting her every day since she started this job. It couldn't get any worse. Could it?

Teresa was the second to arrive. "Morning, Chief. Today's the big day, isn't it? Sterling is coming back to work?"

"Yes, right after he drops Ceylon off at the airport. But he will only ride the desk until he's fully healed."

"It was nice to meet Ceylon at Dirk's dinner party. That girl is going places."

"Absolutely, she is. She's an incredible young woman."

Henry sauntered in next, and his mouth twitched with humor before he schooled his expression. "Morning, Chief. Teresa." He exchanged a look with his coworker, and Emory caught the smile they shared before Teresa stuck her face in a file.

Heat flooded Emory's chest and cheeks. Did the look her deputies share have to do with what had happened between her and Dirk? How could it be, unless Henry said something to Teresa? "I feel like I'm on the outside of an inside joke?"

"No, ma'am. There's no joke. It's just that… how's Sterling doing?" Henry kept the smile off his face, but his eyes danced with merriment.

"He'll be here soon, so as well as can be expected. Haven't you talked to him?"

"Not since yesterday." His mouth twitched.

Irritated at being the brunt of their humor, she confronted him, "So, then you know as much as I do."

Henry looked away, but Teresa shot from the hip. "Hey boss, we're happy you two have finally figured out what Hank and I have known from the first day you took over here."

"And what is that, exactly?"

"The attraction between you two was like a tangible boulder we had to maneuver around." Teresa laughed. "Now maybe we can get to work as normal."

"I'm sure I don't know what you mean." Emory grasped for normalcy. Although she appreciated Teresa's direct approach, she did not want to discuss her personal life at work. "I took dinner to Dirk. So what? I would do the same if either of you were injured."

A laugh burst through Henry's self-control. "Sure. But that was Tuesday. You were still there when I dropped Ceylon off on Thursday." Emory's face flamed, and she touched her hot cheeks with her cool fingers. "Don't feel weird about it, Chief. Like Teresa said, it's about time. We're happy for you guys."

"This topic of conversation doesn't belong at work. Nothing is going to change at the office. I hope you're both comfortable with that."

Teresa bit her lips to keep from smiling and nodded. "More than comfortable, but you're wrong. Things will change—for the better. The huge elephant that's been taking up so much floor space in the office can finally move on."

Dirk's voice registered at the base of Emory's spine, shooting sparks up through her scalp. "I'm glad to see the elephant has left the building." He walked past her and leaned against his desk. "So, what's on the agenda, boss? What's our next most pressing case?"

Filled with gratitude and relief, Emory perched on the edge of Teresa's desk. "Why don't we meet in the conference room in fifteen minutes? I'd like to debrief the Crandall case, and then we can discuss where we are with our other active fugitive searches."

Dirk's eyes softened as his gaze found hers. "Sounds good." He sat in his chair and poked at his keyboard one-handed, working on his report. Henry and Teresa turned to their desks as well, and they moved on with their tasks. Emory released a pent-up breath that reached down to her toes, and her shoulders dropped by several inches. The hard part was over, and it wasn't too bad after all.

———

When Dirk arrived, he gauged the mood in the office, and his heart went out to Emory. Later, he'd give Hank crap for making Emory feel uncomfortable. But at least all the cards were on the table. Now all he had to do was resist touching his beautiful boss while they were at work. His chest swelled with warm emotion as his mind replayed their time together during those incredible days. They'd kept it low-key because of his injuries, and he couldn't wait until he was back a hundred percent. Still, keeping his hands off her was going to be harder than he thought.

When he first stepped into the office, he had casually acknowledged their topic of conversation but pressed on, hoping to give Emory an easy path out of the awkward situation. She had gracefully picked up the ball and set a meeting in fifteen minutes.

Unfortunately, Dirk hadn't had a chance to work on his report on the Crandall takedown. So, he focused on the report at hand. It took forever to get his thoughts on the screen. He wasn't great at typing before, and now with his arm in a sling, the one finger hunt-and-peck slowed him down even more.

Hank looked over Dirk's shoulder. "I've already written a comprehensive report. Why don't you just look at mine and tweak it where you want to? Watching you type is painful and if we wait on you, we'll be here all day."

Teresa chimed in. "Or you could always join the twenty-first century and use the dictation function in Word. Hank, show him how."

"Give a man a break, you two. I'm just noting that I

received a logbook from that old man we talked to in Wyoming. Remember him, Hank? He wrote down all the planes he saw taking off and landing for a month. Not that we need it now."

A knock sounded behind them on the open office door. Dirk swiveled around to see Dave Aldrich regarding him. He stood to face the man. "Aldrich. What can we do for you?"

Dave's eyes bored into Dirk's. "I'm here to see Emory."

"She's in her office." Dirk maintained the powerful stare-down, damned if he'd be the first to blink. Had Emory told him about them? Or did he just assume? "We're debriefing the Crandall case in about ten minutes. Want to sit in?"

That seemed to surprise Aldrich, and he looked away. "Uh, I'll see what Emory thinks, but it might be a good idea."

"I know we'd like to hear what's happened with Crandall since the FBI took him into custody. Besides, you probably have insight from your perspective on the case." Dirk respected Aldrich as a federal agent. He'd always done a good job, and Dirk hoped they could maintain a professional working relationship.

"Thanks." Aldrich pointed at Emory's office door. "I'll just check in with your *boss*."

———

Emory agreed to include Dave in their debrief. Though the air was thick with tension for the first ten minutes, it quickly dissipated as they discussed the details of their recent apprehension. "Looking back at the event, what went well, and what could have gone better?"

Dave drummed the table with his fingers. "From the FBI's perspective, Sterling and Flannigan went in too soon. You guys should have waited for back-up." He pointed to Dirk's sling. "It was reckless cowboying that ended with you getting shot. You're lucky you aren't dead."

"I hear you, Aldrich. And if there weren't children involved, we would have waited. We would have let Crandall get away to catch another day. But we would have lost all those kids forever in the dark world of human trafficking if we didn't move in when we did. Frankly, I'd make the same decision again today. Even if I ended up dead. That's my job. A risk worth taking."

Hank leaned back in his chair. "What took so long for your guys to show up? You should have been there sooner."

"As far as I knew, the Missing Person's Division was on this case. It wasn't until I received the call from Emory that I mobilized the back-up. Now that we know Sheriff Donnelly was working with Crandall, it explains his resistance to federal assistance."

Dirk nodded. "It makes me wonder how deep the corruption goes. Does it end with Donnelly?" He tapped on his phone. "I just emailed you the airplane log from a hobbyist down in Wyoming where the John Doe was found. His report might help you guys out with any investigation down there regarding gun and drug smuggling."

Emory cleared her throat to bring everyone's attention to her so she could redirect their focus. "Let's problem-solve around getting a faster back-up response."

An hour later, she stood, signaling the end of the

debrief. "Dave, when is Crandall's arraignment?" He gave her the court date. "Good. I'd like to be there that day. Other than that, I think we're finished here. Congratulations, to all of you, on a job well done."

She opened a folder and removed three stapled packets which she passed to each of her team members. "I'd like you all to focus on hunting down the wanted fugitives in your packets. We'll meet again at the end of the week for an update. Let me know if you have any questions."

With that, she ended the meeting. She avoided eye contact with Dirk and thanked Dave for being a part of their debrief. "Alright, team. Let's get to work."

EPILOGUE

TWO MONTHS LATER

Dirk ended a call with Sheriff Manning, the Carbon County Deputy who had taken over the position after Donnelly was killed. After typing notes of their conversation, Dirk saved them into his file on Simeon Gryms, the man at the top of his fugitive-hunting workload. He checked his watch, four o'clock. Almost quitting time. He and Emory had fallen into a comfortable stride at work and found that they could maintain a solid professionalism between nine and five. It was a small sacrifice since the hours away from the office burned like Fourth of July sparklers. He couldn't remember ever being so happy.

He was concerned about Hank, however. He was looking haggard and worn thin on most days. Sometimes he shared that he and Amy continued to fight even though their battle with infertility was over. Dirk tried to be there for his partner, but who was he to offer relationship advice? Besides, unless he asked Hank directly, the kid kept his business to himself.

Teresa brought the mail in. She set two envelopes on his desk, and one on Hank's, before taking the rest of the stack into Emory's office. Dirk closed the file he'd been working on and smiled at his screen saver. A photo of Caleb and his Rottweiler, Bear, running through the sprinklers filled his monitor.

An easy friendship had returned between Dirk and Laurie. He saw her and Caleb once a week and tried to take the little guy out once in a while to give her a break. Laurie sent him a text last night saying that she'd run into Dave Aldrich at the movies and that he had asked her to go for a cup of coffee sometime. She had wanted to know what Dirk thought. He avoided answering, wondering why Aldrich couldn't find someone to date that Dirk didn't know.

He also got a message from Ceylon, who was halfway through her first semester at NYU and was killing it. No surprise there. Life was settling in nicely. He sighed and leaned back in his chair. Glancing at his watch, time had only advanced five minutes. The day was taking forever to end. He and Emory had plans to spend the weekend up at his cabin, and he couldn't wait to get on the road. He tapped his boot heel impatiently.

Emory's office door swung open, crashing against the wall behind it. She rushed out and Dirk jumped to his feet. "What's wrong?" Her pallor and the worried expression in her eyes sent cold darts skittering across his skin.

"This came in the mail." She thrust a cardboard box toward him.

Dirk opened the box. Inside, he found a cloth doll with a hand-written note pinned to its head and a zip drive. He unfolded the paper and read. "Sterling, thanks for your part in helping me find my way to paradise. Wish you were here. BC." He looked up in question at Emory. "Where did this come from? No way would they let him send this from prison."

Emory swallowed and rolled her lips between her teeth. Her hand slid over his. "Watch the video on the thumb drive."

Dirk's pulse hammered at his temples as he pushed the memory stick into his computer. An encrypted video loaded. Hank stood behind him to watch along with them. The image of Beaux Crandall's huge bare belly filled the monitor screen until the camera angle panned back. The disgusting pervert waved to them from a cabana on a sparkling white-sand beach. Children played in the sand all around him. A young girl who was maybe twelve, wearing a tropical sarong, served him an umbrella drink, and Crandall slid his hand inside the fabric of her wrap. He laughed as tears ran down the girl's face. Crandall raised his glass in a silent toast, and the video ended.

Fury flooded through Dirk's blood, making it hard for him to draw in a breath. "What *is* this? How can he be on a beach? He's supposed to be in the Supermax in Florence, Colorado."

"I called the warden there as soon as I saw this. Apparently, armed men blocked the road with semi-trucks and forced the bus carrying new inmates to a stop on its way to the prison. They shot the driver and both guards before they helped Crandall escape. They left the other prisoners to their own devices. Police have recovered most of them. That was two days ago."

"Why didn't we hear about this before now?" Dirk knew the answer. He and Emory spent hardly any time watching the news lately. "He must have had his organization running all along. Someone pulling the levers in his absence. This is way bigger than it seemed."

Hank ran a hand over his face. "I thought it was just Crandall and a few men who worked for him."

"Me too, but we were wrong." Dirk wanted to be sick. Those poor kids. "Is there any indication as to where this video was filmed?"

Emory took a tissue from a box on Teresa's desk and pulled the drive. "I'll send it to the FBI analysts. Hopefully, they'll be able to figure it out."

"No." Dirk reacted viscerally to her suggestion.

Emory drew back. "No? Why not?"

"Because Crandall was in the custody of the FBI. And it would have been US Marshals who would have been guarding him during the prison transfer."

"What are you saying?" Emory's face went pale.

"You know what I'm saying. We've got a rotten apple in the barrel—there is someone among us we can't trust. Until we know more, we're keeping this note and video to ourselves." Dirk yanked his leather jacket from his chair. "Come on, Hank. Call Amy and grab your bag. We have some convicts down in Colorado we need to interview." Dirk strode to the door but paused and glanced back at Emory. "Sorry about this weekend. Another time?"

"Of course. Work comes first."

Knowing he'd be gone for several days, he took her

hand, pulled her into her office, and kissed her goodbye—workplace protocol be damned.

———

THANK YOU for reading CORRUPTION!

I hope you enjoyed the thrilling suspense of Corruption, the second book in the US Marshal Thriller Series! The edge of your seat ride continues with REDEMPTION ~ Book 3 in the series.

Order REDEMPTION Now!

REDEMPTION ~ A US Marshal Thriller

In the heart-pounding thriller, REDEMPTION, US Marshal Dirk Sterling faces his most challenging mission yet: capturing the elusive fugitive, Beaux Crandall. Crandall, a criminal with a rap sheet that chills the spine, escaped a life sentence in a Federal Supermax and is now living life somewhere on a beach where he continues his reign of terror: dealing in drugs, guns, and child pornography. Dirk pledges to hunt him down and bring him back to the United States to face justice.

To make matters worse, Dirk isn't sure whom he can trust. Someone on the inside of either the US Marshal Service or the FBI had to have helped Crandall escape. Dirk feels personally responsible for not discovering the mole before Crandall was set free on the world to harm more innocent people. To redeem himself, Dirk must apprehend Crandall and put behind bars for life.

Dirk is determined to end Crandall's evil reign, but the fugitive's location remains a mystery. However, a glimmer of hope appears when Dirk discovers that Crandall's only weakness may be the love he still harbors for his deceased bodyguard and friend's mother, who resides in Mexico City.

In this electrifying tale of love, betrayal, and the relentless pursuit of justice, REDEMPTION takes readers on a thrilling journey where the bonds of friendship, the depths of love, and the quest for retribution converge in an explosive climax that will leave you breathless.

<u>Order REDEMPTION today!</u>

If you enjoyed reading <u>CORRUPTION</u>, I would be forever grateful if you would take a minute to review the book on Amazon.

Thank you!!

For free books and to join my reader group, please visit my website <u>Jodi-Burnett.com</u>

ALSO BY JODI BURNETT

Books also by Jodi Burnett

Run For The Hills

Hidden In The Hills

Danger In The Hills

A Flint River Christmas (Free Epilogue)

A Flint River Cookbook (Free Book)

FBI-K9 Thriller Series

Baxter K9 Hero (Free Prequel)

Avenging Adam

Body Count

Concealed Cargo

Mile High Mayhem

Tin Star K9 Series

RENEGADE

MAVERICK

CARNIVAL (Novella)

MARSHAL

JUSTICE

BLOODLINE

TRIFECTA

US Marshal Dirk Sterling Trilogy
FORGED (Free Prequel)
EXTRACTION
CORRUPTION
REDEMPTION

ACKNOWLEDGMENTS

First, and always, I thank God for blessing me with a vivid imagination, work I love, and for the inspiration with which to do it.

I remain enormously appreciative for my team. I am beyond grateful to Kae Krueger who is the first to see my words and check my stories. A huge thanks to my team of beta readers who help me see the forest for the trees. You all are integral to my writing process. Thank you, Chris, Emily, Sarah, Jenni, Brooke, Sheila, and Kay. Thanks also to my personal assistant, Anna, without whom, I would remain an unorganized fiasco!

I owe a huge debt of gratitude to the US Marshals Service, specifically Deputy Untied States Marshals Andrew Gallagher, Gustavo Marin, and K9 Folly. These deputies generously took time to give a presentation at the Douglas County Sheriff's Citizen's Academy Alumni meeting. Thank you for the abundant information you shared that gave much fodder to this book and more in the future. Thanks to Folly for demonstrating just how amazing police K9 partners can be! Thanks guys!

I'd also like to give a shout out to Dalton Weisshaar, who I can always rely on for correct firearm information. You are a godsend, Dalton! Thank you!

I could not do any of this without the support and encouragement of my family. Writing can be such a solo venture. Thanks for pulling me out of my cave and loving me through the rough spots. I cherish the inside jokes, all the sports, and most especially the way we love each other. My cup overflows.

Most of all, I thank my husband Chris, who helps me flesh out my plots, makes sure my men sound like men, tightens up my military technicalities and lingo, and reads all the words. He listens to my crazy ideas, brainstorms with me, accompanies on my grand adventures, helps me with the business side of writing, and loves me through it all. I rely on his strength and encouragement. I love you, Chris, with all my heart.

ABOUT THE AUTHOR

Jodi Burnett is a Colorado native and a mountain girl at heart. She loves writing Mystery and Suspense Thrillers from her small ranch southeast of Denver, where she lives with her husband and their two big dogs. There she dotes on her horses, complains about her cows, and writes to create a home for her nefarious imaginings. Burnett is a member of Novelists, Inc. and Sisters in Crime. CORRUPTION is her 14th book.